Chimera

Ben Caskey

DEDICATION

This book is dedicated to both my parents who homeschooled me and supported me in my writing. Whether it's helping with cover art or tolerating the long conversations about world building, thank you for all you did. Without you this would not have been possible.

CONTENTS

1 - SCARS

I inhaled sharply as I sprinted through the woods trying to put as much distance as possible between myself and the other hunters. Dead leaves that had spent weeks covered in snow crunched below my feet. It was not hard to smile as I smelled the fresh air which was cool, but not cold as it had been.

Our tribe held a yearly hunt to separate the boys from the men. Each aspiring warrior would go out into the forest to kill an animal. If my father, the chieftain, deemed the kill worthy, then the boy who brought it to him would be accepted into the ranks.

I wasn't worried about whether or not I would be accepted. I was Chimera, the son of the chieftain, as my friends liked to point out. Surely the chieftain would accept his own son's offering. But I was determined to earn my way to success like everyone else. There were rumors of a karcharios in our area, a shark man, as my little brother called them. Anyone who brought down this creature would surely be accepted and any rumors of special treatment for the chieftain's son would be put to rest.

It was a difficult decision, going after such a beast. I was risking either death by the ferocious creature, or if I survived but couldn't kill it, there was no way I would pass the trials. However, it'd been years since a karcharios had been spotted in our neck of the woods. This was an opportunity I couldn't pass up.

The wind began to pick up as I arrived at the clearing that I had scouted earlier. I slung my bow over my shoulder and began to climb the nearest tree. The hunters that spotted the karcharios said he was in this clearing, and it was a popular hunting trail for predators. Little did he know, he wouldn't be the only predator tonight.

I reached my perch just in time because shortly afterward another hunter entered the clearing. The rules of the hunt stated that we could not harm or sabotage another hunter, but I did not want to give my position away and risk someone else getting my kill.

I recognized the hunter to be Apistos, my close friend since I was a boy. We had trained together in the weeks leading up to this but we had kept our plans secret from each other. He was wearing the plain leather armor of our tribe and his short black hair was a mess from his long run through the woods.

I grabbed a rock and threw it farther down the path hoping to lead him away. Not because I wanted him to lose the hunt, but if he spooked my prey then I had no chance at passing the test.

Unfortunately, the rock had the opposite effect. Apistos drew his sword but then didn't move anymore, almost as if he was still working up the courage to go after the noise. My mind was racing trying to come up with ways to make him run off but I couldn't think of anything.

Just then, I heard a petrifying roar beneath me and into the clearing stomped the karcharios I was hunting. Standing at what must have been nearly two feet taller than me, the brute who was half man and half shark had deep blue skin with a fin protruding from the back of his neck.

He was an absolute giant of a creature with enormous muscles from head to toe. The humanoid beast could survive on land or in the water and legends spoke of a time where thousands of karcharios inhabited all of Aragath, though I wasn't sure how much I believed them.

The karcharios charged at Apistos who could do nothing as the beast knocked away his weapon and threw him to the ground. I nocked an arrow on my bow and prepared to shoot my prey in an attempt to save my friend's life. I cursed under my breath when I realized that Apistos had led the creature unintentionally to a place where branches blocked my line of sight. I panicked and hurriedly began climbing back down forgetting all about winning the hunt and more about the danger my friend was in. Apistos cried out for help as the predator moved in on his prey.

Knowing that the creature could rip Apistos in half effortlessly, I stopped descending as soon as I saw an opening through the branches and leaned against the trunk of the tree to steady myself. I nocked an arrow on my bow and carefully measured the wind. I would likely only have one shot at this.

I pulled back on the string and aimed for the back of the karcharios head. I exhaled and then hesitated for just a moment before I released the bowstring and let the arrow fly. I attempted to account for the wind with my aim. My heart sunk when the arrow landed just below the beast's shoulder blade.

The karcharios let out a tremendous roar of pain and turned to face me. I lowered myself the rest of the way down the tree to face the great beast. I brandished my archer's short sword and started shouting at my enemy, drawing him away from Apistos. He began to charge forward in a fit of rage. I waited until he was almost upon me to gracefully sidestep his uncontrolled attack. The karcharios slammed into the tree behind me sending large splinters flying, one of which buried itself in my thigh.

Ignoring the pain I limped over to Apistos who was on his feet and had recovered his weapon. I felt the warm blood running down my leg. It was an injury that could not be ignored for long.

"He can't catch you if you keep moving," I

said, taking a stance next to my friend.

Apistos eyed the karcharios who had recovered and was preparing for another attack. "We should return to camp and get help."

I shook my head. "No, we can do this ourselves."

The karcharios stomped toward us again but we used our speed to keep out of range, swiping at him with our swords but only scratching the beast. We continued to circle our prey waiting for an opportunity to strike but the creature's size made it difficult to get too close. I wiped the sweat from my forehead. It was clear that I should have stayed in the tree.

Realizing the glancing blows were doing nothing against the beast, I sheathed my sword and nocked an arrow on my bow. The karcharios, seeing this, threw himself at Apistos and managed to grab him by the arm and use him as a shield. Apistos wasn't nearly strong enough to resist. I drew back on the bow and aimed but I could not get a clear shot with Apistos flailing about in a futile attempt to free himself.

The battle had come to a standstill, with myself and the beast both weighing our options while Apistos gave up on his escape attempts. As much as I cared about winning the hunt, this was about saving my friend's life now. I held my breath and aimed more carefully than I ever had before. I exhaled and began to let my fingers slip off the bowstring.

Just as I decided to risk the shot, the karcharios hurled Apistos at me and charged. I, however, spun out of the way and loosed my arrow in its direction. I feared the off-balance shot would miss badly, but my fears were erased when the arrow hit its target landing deep in the creature's shoulder and bringing him down to one knee.

I helped Apistos to his feet and then looked at the karcharios who moaned loudly and met my gaze from his place on the ground, clearly struggling to breathe. Blood began to seep both from the arrow in his chest and the one in his back. I could see the pained look in his eyes and I pitied the wounded animal in front of me. I sighed and readied one more arrow to put it out of its misery.

"I surrender," said the karcharios.

His words caught me completely off guard. Everything I had ever heard about the karcharios up to this point was that they were just wild animals. Was it a secret the elders of our tribe were keeping from me? Or perhaps even they didn't know the truth. I kept my bow aimed at his chest wondering if I was imagining things.

"We fought and you bested me," he spoke again. "So I surrender."

I glanced at Apistos still dumbfounded.

"W-what do you want us to do?" I asked lowering my bow.

There was a long pause before he spoke again.

I wasn't sure if he was succumbing to his wounds or simply pondering carefully what to say next.

"I would like you to take me back to your village and tend to my wounds," he said still speaking my language fluently.

I hesitated not knowing whether to listen to him. My goal had been to kill a karcharios and bring it back to my father, but would taking one prisoner be enough? I stood there for some time however I could not bring myself to execute an unarmed prisoner.

Apistos spoke up, "If you bring him back alive you risk not passing the trial."

"And you risk not passing if I tell my father you had no part in capturing him," I said sharply. "We're bringing him back alive."

Apistos sighed and I tied the hands of our new prisoner with the rope I carried. I was no doctor but I knew enough to help remove the arrows from the body of the karcharios. No one spoke as we bandaged them with the little bit of emergency supplies we carried. I waited to remove the splinter from my leg until we had more bandages.

"Don't make me regret this," I said to him.

As we made our way back, the clouds broke and released the first rain of the season marking the official end of winter. The rain quickly turned the dirt path to mud. The karcharios slogged through and we actually had to struggle to get up.

We finally made back it to the village just before dark. The torchlight from the many houses became visible. Our tribe numbered just over two thousand.

I was surprised to see that most of the hunters had already finished. They'd all formed a line in front of my father to present their offerings. Some of them had exotic birds and ferocious wild boar. One student even brought forward a wolf. Meanwhile, others had harmless squirrels, rats, or even nothing at all. The latter would all have to wait until next year to try again.

All eyes turned towards us as we marched our prisoner to the back of the line. Most would be impressed by the capture of the rare karcharios. Others, disappointed by the failure to kill it. When it was our turn, Apistos and I made our way to the front of the line and pushed our prisoner to his knees in front of my father. I knew he could have easily resisted falling if he had wished. Still, I tried to appear confident as I met my father's gaze. On one hand, to offer a karcharios was far greater than anything anyone else had brought. Unfortunately, not only was our gift alive but between the two of us, we only had one offering.

My father was a tall, thin man who had long black hair. His brown skin was wrinkled. He wore elaborate red and brown chieftain's robes. At this moment he appeared quite composed despite the fact that even he had probably never seen a karcharios before.

"Tell me," he said raising an eyebrow, "Why

did you fail to kill your prey?"

I swallowed nervously. For the first time, the possibility of failing this test felt real.

"Because he is not an animal," I blurted out. "He speaks the same language we do."

This made my father raise his eyebrows. He beckoned for the captive to stand and he obeyed.

"Is this true?" My father asked with the kind of excitement that I had rarely seen in the years since my mother passed. "Can you speak?"

The karcharios held his head high and spoke.

"I can," he said holding my father's stare. Despite his state, muddy, wounded, and tied up, the karcharios spoke with authority. He did not break eye contact with my father as if in an act of defiance. His confidence was intimidating, to say the least. Even on his knees, our prisoner was taller than my father. Now, standing, he towered over him. I got the idea that he could have escaped if he really wanted.

"Your warrior bested me," the karcharios said gesturing to me. "I respect that."

My father held his stare and a slight smile crept across his face.

"Very well done, Chimera," he said finally looking away from the magnificent creature before him. "You and Apistos both pass the trials. You are now officially Storm Hunters."

Relief washed over me as the pressure of the last few weeks lifted.

"This karcharios is no longer a prisoner," he

said to anyone who could hear him. "He is our guest."

A few of my father's senior officers stepped forward and my father ordered them to have the karcharios' wounds looked at by a professional.

"Congratulations, Chimera," one of the older ones said.

"Thank you, Syvos," I said, "But I couldn't have done it without Apistos."

Apistos gave me a sideways glance knowing that I was lying through my teeth. Syvos only smiled and continued escorting the karcharios away.

Another of my father's officers, Terros, approached me.

"I won't be impressed until you bring back a dragon," Terros said with mock seriousness in his voice.

Terros was widely known as one of my father's best hunters. He was in his early thirties. He had long black hair that was pulled back into a knot. His arms and face were covered in black paint to conceal him in the dark. To earn his respect was a tall order but one I knew I'd just accomplished. Even a hunter as skilled at Terros had never bested a karcharios.

"Are you going on another hunt?" I asked, ignoring his joke.

He nodded somberly. "Food's low Chimera. Someone's got to do something or we'll all starve. I may be gone for a while on this one."

"Good luck," I said.

"It's the beginning of another storm season," he said moving down the path to rejoin his group. "I don't need luck!"

"Chimera, go have that wound looked at," said my father. The excitement from moments ago was almost completely gone. "You have an hour until the feast."

I nodded and went to do what he said. These feasts were usually more like tribal meetings but maybe now that I passed the trials they would hold a little more interest.

* * *

Thunder boomed loudly as a bolt of lightning ripped across the night sky. The storm continued to intensify and most people had returned to their homes. I wondered how Terros and his men felt out hunting in this weather. Surely with the darkness and the rain, they couldn't see or track anything.

I hustled down the road passing the many straw huts that housed our people. I stopped when I came to the only stone building. It was an old structure built long ago and meant to be a meeting place for the tribe's leadership. I ducked inside through the small wooden door.

In the middle of the room sat a long dinner table that ran the length of the room. The table seated twenty. The back of the room held the kitchen. My stomach growled once I smelled the food. At the head of the table stood my father who was having a quiet conversation with Syvos. No one took notice as I walked up and took my seat beside him.

Most of the table was filled with advisors, military or otherwise, to my father who was the chieftain of the Storm Hunters tribe. Several small round tables surrounded the main one and seated the remainder of the hunters. Though there were a lot fewer hunters present than in past years. Most were out scrounging any bit of food they could find and I hoped to join them soon. If it weren't for their countless hours of scavenging this tribe would have starved long ago.

Next to me sat my twin sister, Rhea, who did notice me and shot a dirty look in my direction for being tardy. And next to her was our younger brother, Anthos, who was barely nine years old and who looked severely out of place in the room full of adults. I smiled for a moment realizing that I could consider myself an adult now that I had passed the trials.

I looked at my bowl of stew and frowned. The beginning of Storm season was the greatest celebration of the year and was usually marked by a great feast. Instead, simply a bowl of stew made from the most meager of rations. I didn't want to seem ungrateful but it was hard not to be disappointed.

No doubt the subject of my father's

conversation would be the unexpected famine our tribe was going through. Usually, we survived the post-winter food shortage by doing more hunting, but a recent earthquake scared most of the wildlife away. The other hunters who passed the trials today and I had gotten lucky. Now we had people foraging for mushrooms and berries, but that was hardly enough to feed our entire tribe.

I looked at the last painting my mother had made before she passed that hung at the end of the room. It depicted the rose oak tree by the river. Underneath the tree was the tombstone for my grandfather whom I'd never met.

The noise made by the rain striking the roof forced everyone to speak very loudly making the entire dining area a very noisy place as we ate. I could smell everyone else's food once I finished which made me wish I had more.

"Did I miss anything important?" I asked my sister as I set about eating the rations in front of me.

"No," she said. "But I hear you got to see something rather special today."

"You heard?" I said excitedly. "Do you know what father plans to do with him?"

"He told me he wanted to recruit the beast to fight for us," said Rhea.

My eyes widened as I recognized the possibility of fighting alongside the magnificent warrior.

"Do you really think he would agree to that?" Rhea asked.

"I don't know, I haven't spoken to him since I captured him. He did surrender so who knows."

Rhea finally started to share some of my excitement and looked like she was about to say something when my father rose to his feet and started to address the room.

"As you all know, our tribe is going through a severe famine. And it's not the usual post winter food shortage," he paused. "This is due to the unexplained shaking of the earth that caused so much of the wildlife to flee far from our lands."

I remembered the horror of a few weeks ago huddled in this very building with my family and many of my tribemates as the ground beneath us shook violently. What felt like hours couldn't have been more than a minute. And though surprisingly little damage could be seen with our eyes, we began to feels the effects as our hunters brought in less and less food.

A wildfire that we attributed to this earthquake destroyed the habitats of many species. Our village was not touched by the fires but animals were leaving in an attempt to find new forests.

"There is a plot of land some distance from here that was discovered by Trofi and his crew," my father pointed towards the proud hunter and many people started to cheer and pound on the tables.

When things quieted down my father

continued. "The land there is soil rich," The people around the table began to look hopeful. "And just as importantly, the area was not affected by the earthquake, so it is teeming with wildlife for us to hunt. I believe this is the prime opportunity for us to settle this land, and start a new village."

"Then what are we waiting for?" A man named Caste shouted and many others began cheering again.

My father held up a hand motioning for them to be silent.

"Unfortunately, as soon as we made this discovery, the Blood Hawks also found out and decided to steal the land out from under us," my father said.

At the mention of our bitter rival tribe, many of the men around the table scowled but began listening more intently. My father had expertly navigated the conflict for years avoiding war with the Blood Hawks the whole way. But always tensions were rising and eventually words would fail to solve things.

"Tomorrow, we ride for Sylvannor to meet with the Sylvan council. They will decide who the land belongs to."

Many of the men at the table groaned and a scrawny young man, who I recognized as one of the hunters who passed the trials last year, stood to speak.

"Why should we bow down to the Sylvan

Council when they give us no aide through this famine?" The young man shouted angrily. "We run around aimlessly trying to please their every desire when we should stand and fight to free ourselves from their rule!"

Syvos stood quickly to defend my father. "And what would you have your chieftain do?" he asked, his face growing red from anger. "March our little army of hunters to the great walls of Sylvannor and demand they surrender? Or would you rather meet them on the battlefield, with our wooden shields and spears, against their army of horse riders and ironwood weapons?"

I glanced at my father who didn't say anything and waited for the situation to play out.

"You know nothing of war, Syvos," said the scrawny man sitting across me. "But how could you?" he asked mockingly. "You're just the medicine man. You look like you've never held a sword in your life!"

The insults were ironic coming from a man of his stature. But tensions were high and I was willing to let things like that go. My father, however, was a different story.

"That's enough!" My father's booming voice startled me. "I will not allow this celebration to be spoiled by trading insults," he said. "We're going to Sylvannor tomorrow. That's my decision."

The room fell silent aside from the howling wind outside. Though they argued, the respect everyone in the room held for my father was clear. He'd never led them blindly into war before. We trusted he would find a way to make peace yet again.

"Chimera, take your siblings back to our home and rest. You will travel with me to Sylvannor in the morning."

For a moment, I felt enthusiasm at the prospect of walking through the great halls of Sylvannor for the first time. But the feeling quickly faded at the bleak mood of the room. I nodded and stood to leave the meeting hall with Rhea and Anthos following behind me.

When we came outside, we noticed that the rain had slowed and the clouds had parted to reveal a full moon. We sloshed through the muddy pathways on the way back to our lodging when I turned off the main road.

"Where are you going?" Rhea asked.

"You wanted to see the karcharios didn't you?"

She raised her eyebrows, surprised I had anticipated her unspoken request, and started after me. We continued down the path for only a short while, with our little brother Anthos tagging along behind us. Before long we came to a straw hut that was guarded by two hunters. Despite my father's declaration that the karcharios was our guest, he still didn't trust the creature alone in our village.

I told the guards my father had sent me and

we stepped inside. The hut was the same as any other we built. One room structures with makeshift cots, they were mostly for sleeping.

The karcharios sat on the floor knowing he was too big for the cot. He was backlit by a torch. I could see that Syvos had tended to his wounds far better than Apistos and I ever could. He wore perhaps the largest pair of leather pants our tailors had ever made but still no shirt as there hadn't been time to make anything that big.

My awestruck siblings came in right behind me. The karcharios opened his eyes and looked at me but didn't say anything. We stared at each other for a long time, neither one of us really knowing what to say. I hoped he did not hold a grudge over our fight but could not tell one way or the other.

Anthos broke the ice for us. "Are you the shark man?" It was obvious he was asking with no ill intent and the look on his face showed genuine curiosity.

The karcharios held a solemn expression for a moment before he allowed what I interpreted as a faint smile.

"Yes," he said in his deep voice. "I am."

I was still amazed by seeing the otherworldly creature speak. The karcharios moved to sit up straighter and winced. His wounds clearly still pained him.

"Sorry about that," I apologized, knowing I had caused his pain. "Do you have a name?"

"Dynam," he said. "It means strength."

I introduced myself and my siblings to him. As I did, my sister grabbed her flask of water and handed it to him. He took it and drank from it greedily but he stopped himself before finishing it.

"Thank you," he said and tried to hand it back to her.

"Keep it," said Rhea.

Dynam nodded gratefully and reached into his shallow pocket to grab a small, silver coin. He gave it to me and I examined it. The coin was clearly ancient and the image had nearly worn off. On one side was the image of a karcharios warrior standing proudly. On the other, a depiction of a majestic bird fanning its wings.

"Is that a phoenix?" I asked raising my eyebrows.

Dynam nodded, "The karcharios and the phoenix were some of the first creatures in Aragath, but far from the last."

Still surprised, I rolled up the sleeve on my left arm to reveal a long scar that glowed orange and yellow and ran across my forearm.

Now it was Dynam's turn to look surprised.

"You were scarred by a phoenix?"

"My father was teaching me how to hunt," I replied. "We came across a phoenix that attacked me and left this mark."

Dynam carefully reached out with a large hand and laid a finger on the scar only to pull back quickly at the burning sensation he felt.

"There are many secrets to the magic of the phoenix that you and I have yet to learn," Dynam said. "Very few individuals have ever received this scar but some believe it is a gift."

"A gift from whom exactly?" Rhea asked.

Dynam shrugged his massive shoulders. "I don't know."

"Do you know anyone else that has this scar?" I asked hopefully.

Dynam grimaced and shook his head. "Yes, I mean... I used to, I think," it was the first time I heard him trip over his words. "But I... well, I can't remember."

I frowned. "How could you forget?"

Dynam continued. "My people's empire was wiped out long before I was born, I spent most of my life living off the land with just myself and my parents, the last of the karcharios. When they were killed by minotaurs..."

He stopped and closed his eyes, he struggled to hold back tears. He paused for a moment before starting again.

"When they were killed, I lost who I was. I became more like the animal you believed me to be. For years of my life, I lived without speaking to anybody. I was surrounded by my anger and grief. My hatred for everything continued to grow, and nothing was strong enough to stop me from killing what I wanted. Your arrow striking me caused me to return to reality. But during that period of animalistic rage, I lost many of my memories of my people, my culture, and even my parents."

I stood there feeling tremendous guilt. Though it did help that perhaps I had unintentionally helped Dynam through my own misguided assumptions.

"Regardless of my story," Dynam said. "I can't imagine you're the only one with that scar. You would do well to seek them out and learn the secrets of the scar."

I realized how tremendously late it was and decided it was time to go. He thanked Rhea for the water and I apologized again for causing his wounds. We returned to the straw hut that we lived in and Anthos fell asleep as soon as he lay on his cot.

My sister and I struggled sometimes to connect with our much younger brother. He was kind and rarely bothered us but we didn't have a lot in common. I made up my mind to spend more time with him when I returned from my trip to Sylvannor.

Rhea went straight to her harp-like instrument and began strumming a soft tune. Her music was well known throughout the tribe and she loved playing for people whenever she got the chance. I used to tease her when we were young about how music was a pointless hobby. But secretly, I was proud of her talent.

I lay in my cot and listened to the low tune as I

thought about the journey to Sylvannor. I had never been to the city before and was thrilled to see something so architecturally advanced. My father had told me stories of all the times he'd visited. He said the walls were impenetrable and the city had never fallen to an invader.

"You really should try singing along with the music," I said to Rhea.

"No," she said looking offended.

"Why not?"

"I have a terrible voice. Besides it sounds better without singing."

"Nonsense, you sound exactly like mother."

The mock argument came to an end at the mention of our mother, Chromia Storm Hunter, who'd died nearly eight years ago to a sickness shortly after giving birth to Anthos. I had finally gotten to a point where I was okay with talking about it. Usually Rhea was, too, but some nights she still couldn't handle it. We both knew, however, that Rhea inherited her love of music from our mother even if it was too painful to think about.

"Why do you think father wants to recruit the karcharios to our side?" I asked.

Rhea shrugged. "Maybe he's anticipating a war with the Blood Hawks."

"But we've never actually had an all out war with the Blood Hawks."

"No," she admitted. "But we've always hated each other and the famine has only made things worse. Don't forget that's the real reason you're going tomorrow. Not only is father negotiating for that new piece of land, but he's also trying to put a stop to anything that could lead to war."

Just as she finished talking my father entered the room and sighed heavily. I could tell from the crease in his brow that he was thinking hard about something. Without a word, he lay down on his cot and seemed to start snoring immediately. Knowing that I had a long day tomorrow I tried to do the same but I was kept awake long after he was by the dreadful thought of war with the Blood Hawks.

2 - BATTLEFIELDS

The rattling sound that the wagon made was constant during our journey to Sylvannor. Every single time there was a root in the dirt path the cart would go crashing over it. The Moulin that pulled the cart was a great, fat four-legged beast that was good for plowing fields but not for traversing terrain such as this. The wagon carried anything we could trade for food. Spare tools, weapons, trinkets. Nothing of true value but food was a resource the Sylvan families had no shortage of.

We had left our camp a few hours before sunrise and our group included me, my father, Syvos, Trofi, Caste, three of my fathers most trusted advisors, and an escort of ten hunters. Each hunter carried a bow and a crudely made short sword. They wore the plain leather armor that I'd grown used to. Even though I saw this trip as an opportunity to prepare myself for becoming chieftain someday, our actual goal was to persuade the council to give us the land we needed to feed our desperately hungry people. My father thought we could last until the first harvest once winter ended but the earthquake put a wrench in those plans.

Before we left my father had advised me to leave all my valuables behind. Sylvannor was the biggest city in the region and there were undoubtedly thieves around every corner. I couldn't think of anything worth stealing other than the coin that Dynam had given me which I left with Anthos. I was worried at first that he would lose it but Rhea assured me that she would keep a close eye on it.

I asked my father if Apistos could come since he too had just passed the trials but he said no. Apistos was disappointed but I promised to describe the city to him in great detail. He punched me playfully in the arm when I said this but I knew he would be eager for details when I returned.

The road to Sylvannor was a straight shot through the forest that took us most of the morning to travel. As we grew closer to the city, the burnt oak trees began to transition into the big and beautiful ironwood trees that made the Sylvan families rich. The trees stood twice the height of any other and were big enough around to live inside of. They didn't burn like oak trees did, but they didn't attract wildlife either. Ironwood was the Sylvan families' greatest resource. They'd mastered the craft of turning the material into the sharpest weapons and toughest armor in all of Aragath. I could see a small group of Sylvan warriors hacking away at one of the trees and my father gave them a respectful nod as we passed.

"So how are we going to convince the Sylvan council to give us the land?" I asked my father.

"Well, first we are going to go talk to a man by the name of Bevan Haldreithan and see if he will take our side," he said.

"And who is that?"

"He is the leader of the Sylvan council and a long time ally of the Storm Hunters tribe. And he is a good friend," said my father smiling. He was clearly reminiscing about some faint memory of his time fighting alongside Bevan in wars of the past. "After that, we'll attend the main council meeting and that's where things will be decided."

There were twelve major Sylvan families that ruled over us and the Blood Hawks. The head of each family has a place on the council. A leader is chosen to rule in the case of war, so the bickering of the council doesn't get in the way of the well being of the people.

My father's expression grew sad. "I was there when Bevan was elected. My father had taken me to go see the ceremony," he said trailing off.

I raised my eyebrows. My father rarely spoke about my grandparents or his childhood in any way. But I had heard from other elders in our tribe that he was not treated well as a boy.

I started to say something but I wasn't sure

there was anything fitting to say at the moment so I remained quiet. What was left of the journey was uneventful but the excited whispers began to travel between the hunters as we approached Sylvannor. A few of the older ones had traveled here before but many were just a few years older than I was.

The dirt path through the woods quickly turned into a beautiful paved walkway. The white brick walls of the city stood as tall as the trees and the brown gates were made of pure ironwood. I heard there was some debate as to whether ironwood was in fact wood, or if it more resembled metal. I'd decided that since it came from trees is must be wood. Although the great brown gates reflected the light the same way as a metal blade would.

Along each side of the gate were long green banners that depicted the symbol of the Sylvan families which was a black scaled dragon blasting fire from its crushing jaws onto a group of valiant archers below.

The lumbering gates stood already open welcoming all traders. The buildings closest to the entrance were smaller but as I looked closer to the city center they grew taller and wider. In the middle of all of it was the council building with its massive pillars standing as a landmark. All of this built from the same white brick that I'd never seen before.

As we made our way inside I was quickly

overwhelmed by the commotion. There were traders all around trying to barter with my father but he just ignored them and pushed through the crowd. These traders attempted to take advantage of everyone who came and went from the city gates by camping right at the entrance. I struggled to keep up while also taking it all in.

There were merchants that sold literally everything I could imagine. Food, tools, weapons, clothes, art, and even pets that ranged from colorful birds to vicious attack hounds. Our Moulin-led cart and the handful of guards around it felt so small in the great city.

There were over a thousand people in the city square alone all trying to complete their own business before the day was over. I noticed they all wore more colorful clothes than our bland brown tunics. It was the first time in my life I felt underdressed. My cheeks grew red. It felt wrong to appear in front of the Sylvan council in what looked like rags next to these people. Some of them were pale skinned, others were darker than I was. I walked past a man who had long red hair tied up into knots around his head. It was simply a different culture than ours was, and one I wanted no part of.

At the end of the crowded main street, we came to the council building. On it, there were twelve massive banners that had the same symbol as the ones outside the gate. However in the center of each one was a different family sigil, representing the twelve Sylvan families. These banners hung from each of the large pillars. I couldn't even begin to imagine how all this was built so many years ago.

My father pointed to the tallest tower on the building.

"That's where Bevan lives and that's where we're going."

We came to another gate that separated the city from the council chambers. A red-haired man with pale skin came out to greet us. He was wearing the chainmail of a knight and had a green tunic overtop that contrasted with his fiery beard.

"Greetings, Andras Storm Hunter," He said addressing my father. "I am Harthor of the Rothruin family. Lord Bevan has ordered me to escort you to his chambers."

Harthor must have had no trouble at all finding us in the crowd with our standout garb. Most of the elegant citizens gave our party a wide berth. My father simply nodded, he ordered the rest of our group to begin trading our supplies. He and I followed Harthor deeper into the castle. Our guide led us through a winding corridor and up a flight of stairs to a small wooden door at the top of a tower.

"A rather humble abode for the leader of the Sylvan families," said Syvos.

"Lord Bevan lives the same as the rest of us," Harthor retorted giving Syvos a sidelong glance.

"He is a good leader."

Harthor opened the door. My father stepped through and I followed. Across the room was a balcony that overlooked the city below. On it was a woman and a boy. Bevan's wife and son, I thought, but did not presume to ask. To one side of the room was a desk covered in tattered documents and books. Sitting at this desk was the man I assumed to be Bevan, who rose to greet us.

He was tall, thin, and wore the green and gold robes of the Sylvan families. He wore a black glove on his left hand. He had long brown hair and his face was that of a young man. I glanced at my father who showed no surprise. Bevan was a man who had fought wars with my father many years ago, so his youth shocked me. However, he had sad green eyes of a man who carried the great burden of leadership.

My father bowed before him and I quickly followed suit but was caught off guard again when I heard Bevan's chuckle.

"Andras, my friends will never bow before me," he said grinning.

My father stood and smiled, but only faintly.

"It saddens me that we meet again under circumstances such as these," my father replied sorrowfully.

The joy quickly left Bevan's expression and was replaced with a far more somber one.

"I know of the famine you face," said Bevan. "And believe me, I have not turned a blind eye."

"Then why have my people not received aid?"

"Because the Sylvan council is filled with some of the most selfish people in this cursed land," Bevan said angrily. "With families like the Gorithans and the Rhobens on the council, I can't get anything done. How their families rose to power, I don't know, but until the sky falls, they won't vote for any law that doesn't directly benefit them."

"But you're their leader, aren't you?" I said suddenly. "Can't you do something about it?"

Bevan's stern look broke when I said that.

"Chimera," he said softly. "I haven't seen you since you were a child."

I stood straight and stared at him as if that would make my words more meaningful.

"I am merely a wartime leader," he said gently. "I cannot overrule what the council says."

My father looked angry now. "Since when do politics get in the way of doing what's right? I thought you were above that."

"And do you think it's right for you to get this piece of land all to yourself?" Bevan asked. "The Blood Hawks are as desperate as you are for food."

"The Blood Hawks are savages!" my father exclaimed.

"My first priority as leader of the Sylvan families is to keep the peace. If I award you the land, Cronus will declare war on you."

I stiffened when I heard the name of the

Blood Hawks chieftain. Cronus used to be a Storm Hunter 40 years ago before he went crazy and murdered my grandfather who had been chieftain at the time. He left with a large portion of our warriors and formed a new tribe, the Blood Hawks.

"Cronus would never do that," my father said.

Bevan raised his eyebrows. "You have not seen him in a long time. He has become unpredictable with age, though he remains ever bold and no less dangerous."

My father looked Bevan up and down. It did not take a genius to figure out that this wasn't what my father expected from this meeting. He looked around the room as if somehow he would find some foolproof argument to throw back at Bevan. There was none.

"If you will not help us then we are done here."

Bevan sighed as my father and I turned to leave.

"Andras," said Bevan as we walked away. "Do not underestimate Cronus. The life that he has lived does not lend itself toward showing mercy."

We joined with Syvos and the rest of our group outside.

"The meeting will begin in about an hour," Harthor said. "Do as you wish until then but don't be late."

As soon as Harthor left, Syvos quickly approached my father.

"How did your meeting with Bevan go?" he asked in a hushed tone. "Is the Haldreithan family with us?"

My father sighed, "Bevan remains an ally, but he will not support us over the Blood Hawks."

"That coward," said one of the hunters and many of the others voiced their agreement.

"Save your insults, they only harm those who use them," my father said. "Bevan is a good man who is trapped by the laws of his people." The group fell silent at my father's words. "You heard Harthor. Meet outside the council chambers in an hour."

And with that, my father started down the hallway. Without his knowing, I casually followed him but fell behind looking at all the magnificent architecture in the hallway. There were great marble statues on either side of the hall depicting various past heroes of the Sylvan families. The vaulted ceilings impressed me the most.

I stopped when I caught up to my father and saw him talking to a man in a metal suit of armor. The man had brown skin and a bald head. He appeared to be in his mid-forties though I was looking at him from a distance. His face was one that looked constantly angry. His armor was decorated with red-tipped, black feathers. I knew this to be the symbol of the Blood Hawks. Why was my father talking to the enemy?

My father seemed to be arguing with the man which made me wonder if maybe he had been confronted. The Blood Hawk jabbed a finger in my father's face. My father shoved his hand away and I wondered if it would escalate any further when Bevan appeared from behind them and made peace. They talked for a few moments before my father turned away and began walking toward me. I narrowly avoided being seen by ducking behind one of the massive pillars.

I waited until my father passed before walking down the hallway to meet back up with my tribe outside the council chambers. When I saw my father he had composed himself. I didn't bother to ask what the topic of their conversation was as we waited for the meeting to begin.

We waited far longer than I expected before Harthor appeared through the door and beckoned for us to come inside. My father strode in first and Syvos and I followed shortly behind him. We found ourselves in a sort of booth in a large white room. In front of us were twelve elevated chairs and in them were the twelve members of the Sylvan council.

The council members all wore green robes with the emblem of their family depicted in the center. I could see Bevan sitting in one of the council chairs toward the center of the room and he looked to be deep in thought.

To our right was another booth identical to ours that was empty. No doubt reserved for the Blood Hawks. Just as we settled in, the door on the other side of the room burst open and in marched the Blood Hawk leaders. They all wore full plate armor with black feathers surrounding their shoulders.

"That is Cronus," Syvos said pointing to the one in front, "Chieftain of the Blood Hawks."

I looked at the intimidating man in the other booth. He had brown skin similar to the rest of our tribe and a bald head. I placed him in his mid-forties. His armor had the Blood Hawks signature display of red-tipped feathers on his shoulders and breastplate. I immediately recognized him to be the Blood Hawk my father spoke to. Why was he talking to the enemy chieftain? Cronus' frown was visible even from my place on the other side of the room. Aside from what he was wearing he could easily pass for a Storm Hunter.

That's because he used to be one I thought but did not say it. "Until he betrayed us."

There was a momentary silence before Bevan stood to address the room.

"Greetings Storm Hunters and Blood Hawks," he said extending his hands towards us. He spoke in a much more formal manner than he had previously to my father. "We are gathered here to discuss the terrible famine that has swept across the land."

Bevan spoke for a short period of time about the protocol for rationing our food, something our tribe had been doing efficiently since the earthquake two weeks ago. Many times he mentioned how he wanted a peaceful end to this conflict and all the council members nodded vigorously.

"But the reason you all traveled here is to discuss the wealthy piece of land discovered by the Storm Hunters," Bevan said. "You seek permission to hunt, grow, and potentially build on this land."

At this many of the hunters in our tribe, including myself, perked up and began listening more intently.

"We will allow both chieftains to make their case to the council. And then we will adjourn while the council deliberates."

There was a slight pause before another member of the council stood. She had long, tangled black hair and pale skin. She was older than the other council members, mid-sixties perhaps. She wore the customary robes of the Sylvan families with the dragon and the archers on the front. However, in the center of that symbol was an ominous black heart. I recognized this to be the sigil of the Gorithan family, meaning this woman was Verissa Gorithan.

"Andras Storm Hunter," she said in a shrill raspy voice. "You have been selected to state your argument first."

My father stood and cleared his throat before speaking. I sighed and prepared myself to hear him repeat the same points he had told me a hundred times before. Mostly he talked about how Terros discovered the land first. He mentioned how the Blood Hawks were uncivilized savages that have broken the laws of the Sylvan families many times. I knew that it was pandering to the members of the council who disapproved of Cronus, but it might just be enough.

My father quickly finished speaking and took his seat beside me. He wiped beads of sweat from his forehead and exhaled slowly. I realized that despite how composed he always seemed he still was not fully used to the politics of being a chieftain. I looked towards Bevan who gave my father a subtle nod of approval.

Bevan rose to his feet once again. "Cronus Blood Hawk, do you have any words for the council?"

Cronus stood and allowed the council to wait patiently before speaking confidently, "Nothing as well rehearsed as Andras' speech."

This drew a small chuckle from a few of the council members who clearly opposed my father. Cronus' voice was deep and menacing. He spoke every word with emphasis that rocked the room.

"But I will ask the council this," he said gesturing towards the seated council members. "Why are the lives of the Storm Hunters more valuable than those of the Blood Hawks?"

"Because your people have chosen to murder and steal their way to power," spoke up Elwin Tenethor, a large man with a long scar across his face.

Cronus held up his hands in mock surrender. "Claims made by those who oppose me that I deny to this day. Besides, even if I am the lying murderer you say, then how am I any different from any of your friends on the council?" Cronus paused before he sat down with a smug look on his face. He had made his point.

I raised my eyebrows and had to restrain myself from laughing. Many of the council members shifted uncomfortably in their seats and Bevan almost appeared to be holding back a smile. No one had ever dared bring up the corruption of the Sylvan council before, let alone to rub it in their face. I was no less hostile toward Cronus but he had just shifted the pressure from his own tribe to the Sylvan council.

I looked at my father who was in a hushed conversation with his advisors. I glanced back to Cronus and frowned. Unless he was a complete fool, why would he say something like that? He did nothing to sway the members that supported us and if anything angered the ones who used to be on his side.

"If the chieftains are finished presenting their case to the council then we will adjourn to make a decision," Bevan spoke swiftly trying to regain control of the situation. My father stood to leave followed by myself and the rest of our group.

We met in the hallway outside the council chambers where my father informed me that the council could take until nightfall to decide. I sighed and sat against the wall next to the other hunters. My father seemed distressed. He knew more about the conflict than I did but after Cronus' outburst, I was hopeful that the council may lean in our favor.

We waited for several hours while the council deliberated. Some of the hunters tried to play games or make small talk but I was uninterested. I could not stop thinking about what we would do if the council did not give us the land. As far as I knew there was no other plan for us. Not getting the land would leave us dependant on traders and merchants, an unsettling thought for a relatively poor tribe.

By the time we reached the third hour, I had nearly driven myself insane thinking of all the bizarre possibilities. If we didn't get the land our people would begin to starve all too soon. It very well could be the end of our tribe. I stood up to go outside and get some fresh air. I glanced at my father to see if he noticed but he was in a hushed conversation with Trofi and Caste.

I exited the building and gasped when I saw an absolutely stunning sunset. The entire sky was coated with fiery orange beams and the few clouds were dotted with streaks of red and purple. It was truly the most magnificent sight I had ever seen.

I heard the door open behind me and I expected that it was my father coming to check on me.

"They say a blood-stained sky is a warning from the gods."

I turned quickly to see that it was not my father but Cronus, chieftain of the Blood Hawks. I stiffened and did not know what to say or do.

Cronus took another step towards me with a faint smile on his face.

"I say that it is a glimpse into the future, a portrait of a battle yet to come," Cronus said walking up next to me.

Seeing that he meant no immediate harm, I turned to look at the sunset again, but this time its beauty was marred by the image of a bloody battlefield. I glanced at Cronus who did not appear to be carrying a weapon. Realizing that the much larger man would not require a sword to end my life, I remained on guard. I couldn't help but feel disdain for the man who had betrayed my people and murdered my grandfather.

There was a brief silence before I realized that he was waiting for a response. I cleared my throat and attempted to speak, but no words came out. I shook my head and took a deep breath.

"That was bold, defying the council like that," I said managing to keep my voice steady.

Cronus' smile disappeared at my response.

"I'm afraid that through my outbursts I may have doomed both our tribes," he said.

"In what way?"

He shook his head. "You will find out soon enough," he said before turning to leave.

"Cronus," I said and he stopped. "Who fights in this battle that you see in the sky?"

His smile returned and he shook his head. "Enjoy your new piece of land," he said before striding confidently back to the council chambers.

I watched him leave and relaxed my muscles when the door finally shut behind him. As the sun fell farther in the sky, the battlefield faded and darkness came upon the city. I tried to shake the image of the bloody battlefield as I turned to leave. I couldn't let that happen, I thought. Somehow my father would achieve peace. He always had.

When I returned to the area where the tribe was resting, I wanted to get my father alone so I could tell him about how Cronus seemingly threatened our tribe. Unfortunately, as soon as I arrived, Harthor came to escort us back into the council chambers. I managed to fall in line before my father noticed that I had been gone.

We entered our booth in the council chambers where we had been only a few hours ago. The twelve council members remained seated in the same way they had been earlier although they seemed far less elegant and much more on edge after three hours of debating.

I looked across the room to see Cronus entering followed by an entourage of Blood Hawk warriors. We made eye contact and he smirked. I quickly looked away trying not to draw attention to the fact that we had spoken. My father looked at me and frowned. He'd noticed Cronus' smirk but didn't understand it.

Bevan rose to his feet to deliver the verdict. His eyes drooped and he spoke less formally than before.

"Storm Hunters and Blood Hawks," he said. "The council has deliberated for some time over who should be given the land. After carefully considering both chieftains presentations we have come to a decision."

I leaned forward in anticipation.

"Due to the crimes committed by the Blood Hawks in the past, we believe it is in the best interest of the Sylvan families and in fact all of Aragath to award the land to the Storm Hunters."

My father let out a sigh of relief sitting next to me and the other hunters were smiling. I wanted to join in their celebration. This should be what ended the famine for our tribe. But I had a sick feeling in my stomach that would not go away.

The Blood Hawks began to exit the council chambers and I looked to see that the last one out was Cronus who met my gaze. He had the same composed look but gave a faint smirk when he saw me. The hair stood up on the back of my neck and I felt an undeniable sense of dread in our victory.

* * *

Syvos and the rest of the hunters were readying the Moulin and the cart for our journey home. Harthor had offered to find us room for the night but my father refused stating that he wanted to return to our camp without delay. Harthor also advised us to leave through a side gate. I didn't think we were in any danger but we could never be too safe.

My father and I were waiting just outside the stables for them to finish loading the cart when I decided to tell him about the conversation I'd had with Cronus. My father, after hearing how he'd threatened our tribe, pursed his lips and turned away from me.

"This is exactly why I didn't want to come here," he said looking at the ground. "I worry not for our safety but for the safety of Rhea and Anthos. And the rest of our tribesmen back home."

I remained quiet not knowing what to say. The pain in my father's voice did nothing to calm my nerves. We stood there in silence while we prepared to leave. Just as the hunters were about finished loading the cart I spotted a black hooded figure coming down the road toward us. I tapped my father on the shoulder discreetly and nodded in the direction of the figure who was nearly invisible in the darkness of night.

The figure continued to make its way towards us hugging the houses and shops that lined the road. It grew closer and closer as I waited for my father to take action. When he was almost upon us my father expertly swiped an arrow from the quiver on his back, nocked it on his bow, and drew it back all in one motion.

"Don't come any closer," he said with a commanding voice.

"Whoa, whoa," a voice came from the cloaked figure and he removed the hood to reveal his face.

I breathed a sigh of relief when I saw that it was Bevan.

"What are you doing here?" my father asked lowering his bow and returning the arrow to its quiver.

Bevan approached us and I could see he held two long items wrapped in cloth.

"I come to bring you a gift and a warning," he said extending one to me and one to my father.

I accepted it graciously and unwrapped the cloth to reveal a magnificent ironwood sword.

I looked up at Bevan as if to ask if he was serious.

"The best smith in Sylvannor finished it just this morning," he said smiling.

"Does it have a name?" I asked.

"No," he said. "The Sylvan families believe that a sword is only an extension of your arm. The weapon is only as good as the one who wields it."

I nodded and gripped the sword for the first time. It was incredibly light and well balanced. I glanced at my father who briefly admired his own new blade before quickly sheathing it.

"And what is your warning?" he said warily.

Bevan's expression quickly turned from happiness to sorrow.

"I have reason to believe Cronus will lead an attack against your tribe and it will be soon," he said solemnly. "I have seen the strength of your people and I believe you can defend yourselves but you must be prepared."

"Your help is still welcome," my father said.

Bevan shook his head. "By the law of the council, I cannot involve myself until after an attack has already taken place."

"By then it may be too late," my father said grimly.

"I do not believe that," Bevan said.

There was a pause before Syvos shouted to my father that they were ready to depart.

"Go now, Andras," Bevan said. "But stay ever vigilant, for war does not wait for the unwilling."

3 - COWARDS

The energy was high amongst my fellow hunters during our journey home. Despite the fatigue of a long day, it was hard not to share in their enthusiasm. After all, the worst obstacle our tribe had faced in years was the famine. Now we no longer had to worry about where our next meal would come from.

Another cause for joy was the pure ironwood blade that hung around my waist. I wanted to take it out and swing it around but I knew that was something a child would do. Still, I knew I would have to show it off when we returned if for no other reason than to make Apistos jealous.

I shivered under my cloak and coughed involuntarily as frozen air entered my lungs. A cold front had caught us all by surprise. It was unfortunate timing for a cold snap but there was nothing to do but press on to the warm fires of home. The swooping winds began to pick up and started to burn my exposed face more and more as we went with the only means of warmth being the torches we used to light the way. I could even see that a very thin layer of snow on the ground in front of us proving that even though winter was officially over, nature didn't always respect our calendars.

"How much farther?" I asked my father.

"It can't be much more than a mile now," he replied yelling over the howling winds even though we walked next to each other.

We continued walking at a slow pace.

"So, what did you think?" my father asked.

"About what?"

"Your first Sylvan council meeting."

I paused to think before answering. It hadn't occurred to me until now but between the celebration of winning the land itself, and worrying about the threats from Cronus, I hardly had any time to reflect on the actual politics of it all.

"To be honest," I said. "It was a little boring."

My father laughed out loud at this causing a few of the hunters to give him sidelong glances.

"That's alright, Chimera," he said. "I too hated politics when I was your age and so did your mother."

I raised my eyebrows. My father rarely talked about my mother. Something about the way the illness took her so quickly, he had never gotten over it.

"I really didn't have a choice but to be involved when I became chieftain," he said moving on quickly. "Someday this responsibility will be forced upon you the same way it was for me."

I wrinkled my nose. Being a chieftain didn't sound so bad but I would much rather be a warrior on the front lines than to deal with politicians.

"I understand how you feel about it right now," my father said. "But we needn't worry about the future until it is upon us."

He squeezed my shoulder and we continued down the dark trail.

A few minutes later the Moulin strayed too far to the right and a wheel became stuck on a tree root. The tired beast was not strong enough to pull it through. Not wanting to take the time to unload the cart or even send a messenger to camp to call for help, my father commanded the hunters to line up on each side of the wagon where we would try to lift it up over the root. Bevan had sent us home with a small amount of food, so the cart was lighter than it could be, but even that was going to be hard to lift.

"On my mark!" My father shouted so he could be heard over the wind.

I positioned myself to lift the cart and hoped that my numbing fingers wouldn't drop it.

"Lift!"

At my father's call, I tried lifting with all my strength. It was just beginning to rise when I heard several thuds mixed in with screams on the other side of the cart. Fearing that one of the hunters had dropped it on his leg I rushed to the other side but when I turned the corner the sight I saw was much worse.

All three advisors, five hunters, and Trofi lie dead on the ground pierced by arrows. It seemed like there must have been nearly a hundred flaming arrows protruding from the side of the wagon. The horrific sight of the wounded or dead hunters made my stomach turn and I couldn't seem to move.

I could hear the terrible groans of the injured hunters. Trofi, who was on the ground in front of me, was still alive. He reached out a bloody hand toward me as if pleading for help. I froze seeing a pair of arrows protruding from his chest and did not know what to do. Before I could make up my mind, my father pulled me back behind cover just as another wave of arrows crashed into the wounded men on the ground silencing their moans.

Those of us who were still alive took cover behind the cart which shielded us from the arrows but also kept us from seeing our attackers. Next to me were my father, Syvos, Caste and five other hunters I did not know. The rest of our group had been murdered. I saw one arrow that had landed in the tree in front of me had black fletching with red on the end. The sign of the Blood Hawks.

I clenched my fist and slammed it into the wooden wagon. The cowards had ambushed us while we were defenseless. I nocked an arrow on my bow and waited for the thud of another volley. As soon as I heard it I whirled around and loosed my arrow wildly into the forest on the hill and then took cover again before I could see if I hit anything.

I started to hear the Blood Hawks whooping and screeching their battle cries. Drums began to pound and I was beginning to realize the scale of this ambush. They weren't leaving anything to chance and they weren't taking any prisoners. If they charged at us, it would be over in minutes. My father barked out an order to nock another arrow.

"Draw!"

I pulled back on my bowstring and stepped back to aim over my cover.

"Loose!"

I released my bowstring and my arrow shot forward parallel to the arrows of my tribesmen. The seven arrows quickly disappeared into the forest and it was unlikely any of them found the hearts of our enemies. We ducked behind cover just before another hailstorm of burning arrows came crashing down around us and we realized just how vastly we were outnumbered.

"Chimera!" my father cried. "Get back to the village and find your brother and sister!"

I hesitated. I didn't want to leave my father here to die. I heard the sound of the Blood Hawk battle cries getting closer and the sound of heavy footsteps crashing down the hill. I looked at my father as he shot another arrow. He was a great warrior, but this battle did not look winnable.

"Go now!" my father said drawing his new ironwood blade. "Find them and protect them!"

I nodded and began backing into the woods. Just as I got to the edge of the forest I turned back to see Blood Hawk warriors charging down the hill toward where my father and his allies crouched waiting for their last battle. In the middle of all of them was Cronus who wielded a great broadsword and looked terrifying.

Knowing that there was nothing I could do to help them anymore I turned and started sprinting through the woods towards our encampment. I felt as though my heart was being torn out as I ran away. I could hear the clashing of steel blades and the screams of dying soldiers behind me. I tried to blink back tears and focus on my own mission. Hopefully, I would make it in time to warn the rest of my tribe and prepare our warriors for battle.

I quickly grew winded sprinting through the frozen forest. My lungs burned as they filled up with cold air. I wanted to slow down but I couldn't risk the Blood Hawks beating me there. I made a push to run faster but I tripped over a root and went flying into the mud and snow. I lay still for only a moment looking around at the burnt stumps. I could still hear the distant sounds of battle and whether they were real or imagined, they motivated me to pull myself back to my feet and force my legs to continue running.

In the distance, I could see several lights through the trees. I was getting closer. I continued to run until I came out of the forest and I could see the village below. It was exactly as I feared. The lights that I had thought were from campfires were in reality huts that had been set ablaze.

I could see Blood Hawk warriors marching down the paths executing anyone who dared to put up a fight. A few hunters volleyed arrows at the warriors but they merely plinked off the heavy plate armor that the Blood Hawks wore. I scurried down the hill now completely out of breath and made my way towards the meeting hall where I hoped to find my two siblings. Being the only building made out of stone it was easily the most defensible and a good place to start looking.

I crouched along the path trying to keep out of sight of any Blood Hawks still in this area. I winced as I saw the bodies scattered around, their blood staining the fresh layer of snow. Very few of the deceased were Blood Hawks, I noticed. I ducked into a hut quickly when I saw another two-man patrol coming. This time they were rolling a barrel along with them.

I carefully followed behind them and noticed a cloud of light red dust was leaking from the barrel.

Dragon dust, I thought biting my lip.

The extremely explosive substance was said to be shaved from the very scales of a dragon and was extremely rare. I had no idea how the Blood Hawks could have gotten their hands on even a fraction of the dust, let alone enough to burn our entire encampment.

The two soldiers came to a tent that had been untouched and began to haul the barrel inside. I quickly nocked an arrow on my bow. I tore a piece of cloth from my shirt and wrapped it around the arrowhead before running toward a burning hut across the path. I dipped the tip of my arrow in the flame igniting it, then raced back to the hut with the patrol inside. I poked my head through the door just long enough to locate the barrel, draw back my bow as far as I could, and release the bowstring.

The barrel erupted in a fiery explosion on contact. I was thrown backward by the force of the blast and landed on my back. The two Blood Hawks screamed only for a moment before being killed instantly. Even their big bulky suits of armor could not save them. Though grim, it was satisfying to claim a small victory in what had otherwise been an extremely one-sided battle.

I came over the hill to see a large group of Blood Hawks surrounding the meeting hall. They huddled near the entrance as if they were spectators to a fight inside. I felt the fear creep up my spine but I suppressed it quickly. I clenched my teeth and nocked an arrow on my bow. My brother and sister were in that building and I was going to get them out or die trying.

I loosed the first arrow which landed in the neck of a Blood Hawk soldier. When they saw the death of their comrade, four more turned to face me brandishing their broadswords. I quickly loosed another pair of arrows downing two more foes. I drew my ironwood blade and prepared to engage the remaining two warriors.

The enraged Blood Hawks swung their swords wildly at first making it easy to parry and dodge their blows. But after a few moments, they became far more focused and in sync with each other. My opponents swung towards me at the same time and I parried the sword that would have taken my head but could not evade the blade that cut deep into my stomach.

I screamed out in pain and kicked at the soldier who had wounded me sending him sprawling backward. While I was distracted, the other warrior tried to bring his sword crashing down on me. I narrowly sidestepped the lethal attack and plunged my own sword through the breastplate and straight into the abdomen of my foe. The man and I were both surprised that the ironwood sword was sharp enough to penetrate the heavy plate armor of the Blood Hawk warriors.

The final soldier had regained his footing and came charging at me but before he could even get close I switched back to my bow and nocked an arrow. The soldier stopped running toward me and in fact started backing away slowly. I kept my arrow aimed for his neck. The soldier quickly turned his back to me and started running away.

A small part of me wanted to kill him anyway. He and his people had come to our home and murdered my tribesmen. The odds were high that the cowardly soldier had just today killed someone that I had known my whole life. I hesitated for only a moment longer before the fleeing soldier was almost undoubtedly out of range. Angry at the fact that I had let him go I released the arrow in his direction and to my surprise, it landed just a few feet short of him. The soldier yelped and began running faster.

I looked around at the four lifeless bodies. Moments ago they were alive but now I'd taken that away from them. I'd never killed anyone before and it was by no means something I enjoyed doing. Perhaps if they truly were murderers then they deserved it. But in the same vein maybe I was no better than they were.

Remembering my mission I entered my father's tent which was no less cold than the outdoors. To my surprise, the bodies of Blood Hawk warriors littered the floor. I could not see a single deceased Storm Hunter. Where were the hunters that had been assigned by my father to defend my siblings? Surely they had not fought off the Blood Hawks without casualties.

At the end of the long tent, I could see the few

remaining Blood Hawks fighting a large beast. The creature lifted one of the Blood Hawk warriors, plate armor and all, and punched him square in the chest. The beast then hurled the warrior across the room towards me. The warrior crashed into the ground next to me and I could see that his breastplate had been completely collapsed and no doubt so had his chest.

I aimed my bow at the distracted soldiers and approached slowly. When I got closer I was shocked to recognize the beast. It was the karcharios prisoner, Dynam. He was noticeably taking a defensive position in front of my sister, Rhea, who was clearly shaken.

I loosed an arrow into the back of one of the attackers. Dynam noticed me creeping up behind them and let out a tremendous roar. The remaining Blood Hawks turned to flee but they ran right into my sword. I dispatched them quickly and turned to face Dynam again.

The giant beast breathed heavily from the fight and his bare chest was covered in gashes from his opponent's blades. The wounds that I had given him only a day earlier had reopened and would need immediate medical attention. It didn't take more than a glance around the room to see that Dynam had fought off at least thirty fully armored Blood Hawk warriors by himself.

My sister ran toward me and we embraced. I was relieved to have saved at least one of my family members today. Just then I felt my stomach drop and I backed away from my sister.

"Rhea," I said slowly. "Where is Anthos?"

The fraction of happiness that I had felt for just a moment was shattered again at the tears in her eyes. Was he dead? Had my only brother been killed before I had arrived?

"They took him," Rhea said avoiding eye contact.

I should have been relieved to hear Anthos wasn't dead. Instead, I felt only anger. I exhaled slowly trying to calm myself, but on the inside I was fuming.

"What happened, Chimera?" Rhea asked quietly. "Where is Father?"

I closed my eyes but I could not hold back the tears that rolled down my cheek. I turned and sat on a nearby bench. I was beginning to feel lightheaded.

"The Sylvan council gave us the land," I said sorrowfully. "We had won until the Blood Hawks ambushed us on the road. We didn't stand a chance."

Rhea sat next to me and put a comforting arm around my shoulder. We waited in silence for a few moments.

"Where are the rest of the Storm Hunters?" I asked. "Why was Dynam the only one defending you?"

"They retreated," Dynam said. "As soon as the Blood Hawks came they fell back to the western side of the camp."

"Who ordered the retreat?" I asked clenching my fist.

Dynam hesitated before saying, "Apistos."

I stiffened. How could Apistos take command of the Storm Hunters? Even more importantly how could my best friend leave my brother and sister behind?

"Your people were scared and most of the elders were killed," Dynam said. "Apistos rallied them to retreat and regroup in the back half of the encampment. He brought as many people as he could but in the chaos-"

I held up my hand for Dynam to stop talking. Maybe what Apistos did was the right move at the time, but he still left my two siblings to almost certain death.

"Chimera, Apistos may have saved the tribe from being completely wiped out," Rhea said.

I held my head in my hands and let the events of the day sink in. Rhea set about using what little Syvos had taught her to tend Dynam's wounds. I stared at the blood that covered my tunic and desperately tried to wipe it off to no avail. I didn't regret killing to save my siblings, but it was shocking all the same.

We remained there only until Dynam caught his breath before setting out to find the survivors. When we exited the hut I could see the sun peeking over the horizon. Rhea and I had to help Dynam every step of the way because of his wounds but it was not irritating at all. Dynam deserved every luxury and honor we had left to give.

When we had walked a considerable distance I saw a makeshift barricade with several archers placed around it. I recognized them as Storm Hunters and when they saw who we were they let us in immediately. We helped Dynam get to the medical tent that had been hastily set up after the attack and he lay down next to the many other wounded soldiers.

Rhea went about helping the healers tend to the injured. I looked around at the group of people remaining in my tribe. Though there were more survivors than I expected, there were still a lot of missing faces.

Many people ran past me, some with bows going to the barricade, others carrying buckets of water to fight the growing fires. As I looked at the bustling crowd my head began to spin and I began to feel uneasy. I tried to take a step towards something I could use to steady myself but as soon as I did I collapsed and fell unconscious.

* * *

When I awakened I was lying on a mat inside a hut. I was curiously on my own and not surrounded by other wounded soldiers like I thought I would be. I wondered for a brief moment if the Blood Hawks had come back and captured me. I tried to sit up but immediately felt a sharp pain across my stomach. The wound I suffered from fighting the Blood Hawks was most likely what caused me to blackout.

On the other side of the hut, I could see my sword and my bow propped up against the wall. I grunted at the throbbing pain as I tried again to get to my feet. I managed to do so, but not without great agony. I made my way over to pick up my sword and just as I did I heard footsteps at the entrance. I quickly swung around to point the blade at the intruder, but I was relieved to see that it was only Apistos coming to check on me.

He only held his hands up as if to show that he meant no harm. I lowered my blade and Apistos continued into the tent.

"How long was I unconscious?" I asked trying to look past him.

"It has been about a day and a half since the attack," he said.

I said nothing and only stared at the ground. The chances of finding my father were significantly lower this long after the attack even if he was still alive.

"Why did you leave them?" I said.

Apistos looked at me surprised but then avoided making eye contact, "I tried to get to them Chimera, but the meeting hall was swarming with Blood Hawks."

"Dynam got to them," I said jabbing a finger in his face. "If you had tried harder then maybe my brother wouldn't be a hostage right now!"

"Dynam is a creature of legend, a myth!"

Apistos retorted, "And if it wasn't for me then we would have lost a whole lot more people to that attack."

We stared at each other both angry over what had happened and taking it out on each other. I knew Apistos had saved our people but I couldn't get over the fact that he abandoned my brother and sister. I took a half step toward him intending to get in a fight but the pain from my wound stopped me.

"The Blood Hawks retreated and left the camp shortly after we found you blacked out," Apistos said. "When you've cooled off, come to the war room where we will discuss our next course of action."

Apistos turned to leave but stopped in the entrance.

"For now Chimera, you are the acting chieftain of the Storm Hunters."

4 - ANGER

When I exited the hut a light rain was falling from the sky and the wind was calm. Steam rose from the side of the camp that had been destroyed as the rain hit the still hot coals. The general panic that filled the air just before I passed out was gone, now replaced with an uneasy sense of normalcy. But nothing about this was normal. We were at war for the first time since my father was my age, and our true chieftain was missing.

It took me longer than I expected to get to the new war room. Though the meeting hall was still intact, it was surrounded by bodies and ashes of homes. When I came to the war room I recognized it as the hut that housed the Anastas family. A happy young couple who had two young girls. I wanted so badly for them to be okay but nothing good could have happened if we had already repurposed their home. I shook my head and tried not to think about it.

When I entered the hut I could immediately sense it was far less formal than these meetings were under my father. Inside there were merely four chairs, three of them already seating Apistos, Rhea, and Dynam. They were in deep conversation when I arrived, though they stopped when I sat down. Someone had laid out a small bowl of stew ahead of time and I eagerly partook. I was ravenous having not eaten in days.

I studied the room, a meeting that usually would include all of my father's top advisors and now there were only four of us. Rhea, who took over for Syvos as the lead healer. Apistos, who I was still struggling to forgive. And Dynam who had proven his loyalty but did not yet know our ways. All the elders had been slaughtered as had most of our experienced hunters. It almost felt wrong to make any decision that would affect the entire tribe. I was not happy with our odds.

We had hardly begun the cleanup, but looking at the survivors we had about 100 hunters left not including the ten that Terros took on a hunt with him. And I didn't want to give up hope on my father either. I made a mental note to make sure Terros was at the next meeting when he returned. He had a tendency to be on a hunt for days at a time but he could add an experienced voice to our ragtag council.

Rhea broke the silence, "I think you should start by telling us what happened in Sylvannor, Chimera."

I took a deep breath before I started, "Everything went as planned. Father convinced the Sylvan council to give us the land and they did." I shook my head. "We were ambushed during our return trip. As far as we know father and his advisors are all missing or dead."

Nobody in the room made a sound as we all registered that our entire tribal leadership might have been completely wiped out in one day.

Apistos was the one who broke the silence. "The way I see it, we have two options," he said. "The first option is to declare war on the Blood Hawks, something that I believe we are incapable of after our performance during the attack."

I realized as he said this that war seemed to be the only possibility I had considered up to that point. Now after seeing how the Blood Hawks destroyed our few soldiers perhaps Apistos was right.

"The second option," Apistos continued, "would be to go to the Sylvan council and plead our case. They awarded us the land. Who says that they wouldn't punish the Blood Hawks for the injustice they've done to us?"

"But what about Anthos?" Rhea said, "Will the Sylvan council really prioritize getting our brother back?"

"Maybe not," Apistos said. "But if nothing else they could buy us time to help our wounded and prepare our defenses. Right now we are vulnerable and our enemy knows that."

"We could move to the new land and try to hold our ground there," Rhea said.

Apistos shook his head. "We can't trust

ourselves to protect our people on the road. If they attack us again we would be wiped out."

Apistos seemed to be controlling the meeting. He hadn't necessarily said anything wrong yet, but I wasn't a fan.

Dynam, who had been quiet this whole time spoke up now.

"What would do you believe your father would do, Chimera?"

I sighed knowing they looked to me to make the decision though I did not want to.

"My father trusted Bevan," I said. "He would go to the council for help."

"What's to stop the Blood Hawks from attacking us as soon as we are on the road again?" Rhea asked cautiously.

"We can stay just inside the tree line," Dynam said. "It guarantees nothing but will provide concealment."

"Alright, but we move quickly. I want to be back here before nightfall," I said.

Part of me was still hesitant about this, but traveling back to Sylvannor would give us a chance to search for Father again. And that was a risk I was willing to take.

"Then we should leave at once," Apistos said.

I left the hut to go prepare myself for another journey when Apistos caught my attention.

"Where'd you get the sword?" he asked.

I looked at him warily. Perhaps he was trying to mend our relationship but it was just too soon.

"It was a gift," I said holding his gaze.

Normally Apistos would be jealous but he remained somber.

"Chimera, you have to understand-"

"Understand what?" I threw the words back in his face. "Understand that it was too dangerous for you to try and save my brother's life?"

"I saved half of this tribe Chimera, I couldn't risk them just to save two people," Apistos said his face turning red.

"You left them to die!"

"I'm not the only one though am I, Chimera?"

I set my jaw and stared at him. I knew he didn't mean what he just said but it didn't change the fact that he said it. I turned around and stormed off knowing that the argument accomplished nothing.

I followed Rhea back to our hut to prepare myself for another journey. We were one of the lucky ones whose home was on the safe side of camp. I'd kept my sword by my side the whole time since the attack but we still needed to gather rations.

"You shouldn't blame Apistos for what happened," Rhea said without looking up from her packing.

"I know," I said. "I understand it's my fault Anthos is gone. It's also my fault that Father is dead."

Rhea jerked around with a frown on her face. "I don't think any of that is true."

She sat down on the cot next to me and placed a comforting hand on my shoulder.

"You'll see," she said. "Father will have survived and he'll help us get Anthos back."

I stared at the ground. I liked what my sister said but the chances were not good. The Blood Hawks had brought an overwhelming force and my father was not the kind of man to run from a fight, even an unwinnable one. Nevertheless, Rhea's comforting words encouraged me.

I stood up and finished packing my bag without another word. The quicker we got on the road the higher the chance we would find my father. It took less than an hour for us to gather a five-man escort of hunters to travel with us. I commanded the remaining guards to keep watch at all hours for Blood Hawks. So we set out towards Sylvannor for the second time in as many days, hoping desperately for a happier ending than we got last time.

Our group was quiet as we traveled. No one was optimistic in light of the tragedy we just faced. I struggled with my new responsibilities. So many lives now depended on me to lead them to safety. I hoped that somehow my father had defied all the odds and defeated the Blood Hawks. I hoped that he would come walking down the path any minute now and show me the way to fix everything that had gone wrong.

I knew when we were approaching the place where we had been ambushed and I felt sick to my stomach with nervousness. We exited the woods and I could see the distant cart in the middle of the path. As we approached I caught sight of the gruesome scene.

The ground was still stained with dark red blood and the bodies of my tribesmen were strewn about. They were not only cut by swords or pierced by arrows, but they were also gutted in the most brutal way. Many of the bodies were torn wide open and it appeared that they had been feasted on by some horrific beast.

I concentrated hard on not vomiting due to the smell. I gingerly stepped around corpses trying to avoid stepping in anything. I could hear the buzzing of the blood flies as they feasted upon the decaying flesh. The Moulin that had pulled our cart was particularly disgusting. Its entire left side had been torn open and the insides of the poor beast were falling out. I peered into the cart that carried all our belongings only to find that it had been looted by the Blood Hawks.

"What kind of creature did this?" Apistos asked.

I shook my head not knowing what to say. I slowly walked through the scene of the bloody massacre trying to identify the dead. I saw Trofi and Caste whose bodies had been so disrespected after death. I felt immense guilt knowing that I had run away in their last moments to save my family instead of fighting and dying alongside them.

I held my breath before kneeling down beside one of the bodies. My heart sank when I saw that it was Syvos, the kind old man had done nothing to deserve this. He had obvious wounds in his chest which had been ripped wide open, but I could see in his shoulder was the telltale mark of an arrow wound. I stood up realizing what had happened here.

"These men were murdered by Blood Hawks," I said. "But after the battle, they dressed the scene to make it look like they were mauled by some vicious animal."

I clenched my fist at the severe injustice that had been done to these brave men who in their last moments fought and died with honor.

"This is the work of a monster!" Rhea said angrily.

I noticed Apistos too was turning red in the face and knew he was thinking the same thing I was. Why wasn't I there to help these men?

"Chimera," Dynam said quietly. "The Blood Hawks will spin this to avoid any repercussions from the council."

I realized he was right. As brutal as Cronus seemed, there was a calculated side to him that was truly terrifying to me. Somehow he was in complete control despite the fact that the Sylvan council ruled in favor of the Storm Hunters.

"We must get there quickly," I said.

I thought if we could get to the council before the Blood Hawks did then they would have a better chance of believing our story. Though our odds were not good it may be our best chance at getting justice.

We hurriedly moved through the scene of the crime when I spotted another body behind a tree ahead of us. I moved swiftly toward it. I got closer when I saw that it was in fact, the body of my father. Perched up against the back of the tree my father had the same sickening wounds that the other soldiers had. I felt like I'd just been punched in the gut. I slowly approached his body, tears flowing freely now as the dream of my father coming back to take the burden of being chieftain away was shattered. Rhea came just a moment after and she too broke down at the sight. No one said anything as we mourned our dead father.

There was no gentle breeze as we grieved. No comforting words from one of the elders to lessen our sorrow. Only the unnerving stillness of the woods and the buzzing of the blood flies. Dynam allowed us more time than he should have before placing a gentle hand on my shoulder.

"Chimera," he said in as soft a voice as a creature of his size could. "We have to go."

I nodded slowly before standing.

"Apistos," I said wiping the tears from my eyes. "Take a few men and bring the bodies back to camp. Bury my father under the rose oak next to his father."

I looked around his body for something to remember him by but noticed the ironwood blade that Bevan had given him was gone. I looked around briefly but could not find it. Rhea and I backed away so Apistos could collect the body and load it into the cart. We watched as he and four other hunters walked down the path back to our encampment with the bodies of our fallen comrades.

The rest of the journey was nothing short of miserable. Just like before, no one said a word, but the silence had become far more ominous. I walked in the front of our group, away from my allies and away from my sister. I knew it was wrong, shutting her out like that, especially when my sister was grieving just as much as I was but I couldn't help it. I was just so angry at the cowardly attack that led to the death of my father.

As we got closer to Sylvannor I became unsure of what I planned on doing when we arrived. I knew that the Blood Hawks would be spinning a tale of how they just happened upon the bodies of my father. I figured I would go to Bevan first and tell him the truth about the ambush.

I tensed when a felt a large hand on my shoulder. I turned to see that it was Dynam. I didn't want to discuss my father's death but I wasn't going to completely ignore his kind gesture.

"I was in a very similar position to yours when my parents were murdered," Dynam said.

It hurt to be reminded again of the loss, but I tried to ignore it.

"I made the wrong choice and became filled with rage for much of my life. That is the event that turned me from an honorable karcharios into a wandering beast."

He paused gauging whether I wanted him to continue. I did.

"When I saw the Blood Hawks attacking your sister, I knew it was my chance to save you from the same grief that ruined me. I only wish I could have saved your father as well."

I owed so much to Dynam. If it weren't for him then Rhea surely would have been taken alongside Anthos.

"Chimera," Dynam said, "do not become consumed with the desire for vengeance like I did. It is more dangerous than any sword and can ruin your life."

Those words hit hard. Ever since the attack, I had been thinking about revenge more than anything else. But I could not ignore Dynam's words of wisdom.

"I also can't deny I'm curious to know the secrets of your scar myself."

I glanced at my arm and noticed the faint glow through my sleeve that you could only see if you were looking for it. It truly was unlike anything I'd ever seen before and I secretly hoped that he was right about there being some sort of hidden power within it. If it could somehow be used as a weapon against Cronus that could give us the edge in a crucial battle.

There was no one harvesting the ironwood trees as we passed through the forest. In fact, it looked as though the site had been abandoned. Tools were left lying around as if the workers left in a hurry. I wondered if the council had already heard of the attack and pulled their people back inside the walls. Cronus may have beaten us there.

When I saw the great walls of Sylvannor through the trees I didn't feel awe like I did on my first visit. This time I felt only nervousness. I could see just outside the towering gates was a small line of people waiting to enter the city. This time the gates were closed and everyone entering the city had to be checked by the guards. I noticed there were far more guards than on my previous visit and they all seemed to be on edge. Archers lined the high white walls with a perfect view of the entire field in front of the city.

"Was there this much security two days ago?" Rhea asked.

"No," I said pursing my lips.

We stayed calm and fell in line behind the other guests. As soon as we did, a tall guard who appeared to be the captain came towards me wielding a loaded crossbow. He had dark skin and a scowl that might rival that of Cronus. On his chest was the green emblem of the Sylvan families and in the center of that was the depiction of two crossed swords. This I recognized to be the sigil of the Tenethor family.

"Who are you and what is your business in Sylvannor?" the captain said.

"We are the leaders of the Storm Hunters tribe and we are here to meet with the Sylvan council," I replied.

The captain raised his eyebrows at me and smirked. I realized that our group did not resemble the leaders of the Storm Hunters two days ago.

"I doubt you will gain an audience with the Sylvan council," the captain said. "What are you doing with that monster?" I tensed as he gestured towards Dynam with his crossbow.

"He is an ally of mine and extremely trustworthy," I said.

The captain shook his head. "Well, he's not coming into Sylvannor.

I clenched my teeth and tilted my head. "He's one of us," I said trying to stay composed.

"Not anymore," the captain gestured and two other guards came forward and tried to tie Dynam down.

"Hey!" I shouted at the guards.

They didn't stop so I ran up to the captain and tried to pull him off Dynam. He whirled around quickly and shoved me to the ground. He drew his sword and pointed it right at me.

"Stay out of this, boy," he said.

Angry and panicked, I commanded the Storm

Hunters who raised their bows towards the guards that held Dynam on the ground. In response, many of the guards raised their hands.

The captain raised his sword and pointed to the top of the walls where archers now stood aiming at my fellow tribesmen. I held my breath in fear, one soldier slipping and letting their arrow fly would cause the release of every other arrow.

"If a single arrow flies toward me and my men," the captain said. "Then half of the Sylvan armies will descend upon you."

I slowly got back on my feet and brandished my own sword at the captain. Though the guards had released him, Dynam remained on the ground and out of the way of the standoff. I glanced to the top of the walls to see what must have been nearly twenty archers lined up with their bows trained on me and my people. My heart was racing as I watched the standoff, no one making a move.

"Stop this madness!"

I turned around to see Harthor stomping towards me. At his back were a handful of his own guards with their swords drawn. I began to address him but he pushed past me and approached the head guard.

They spoke in hushed voices but I happened to be near enough to hear.

"What are you doing apprehending that creature?" Harthor said pointing an accusing finger in the guard's face.

"He fits the description perfectly," the guard replied. "We were trying to stop a monster from entering the city."

I looked at Dynam who did not react, whether he heard or not I couldn't tell.

"So now you take orders from criminals!" Harthor shouted at the guard. "Lower your weapons, all of you."

I signaled to my tribesmen to stand down and the Sylvan guards did the same.

"Come with me, Chimera," Harthor said with a scowl on his face as he stormed back inside the city.

I followed behind them and the rest of my tribesmen came after me. The captain of the guard sneered at Dynam but released him. We followed Harthor into the bustling city.

"Why would they try to arrest you?" I asked Dynam.

He didn't respond for a moment. But I could tell he wasn't thinking of what to say, just whether or not he should say it.

"I think they believe that I am the one who ambushed you and murdered your father," he said.

"But that's not true!" I said my face turning red. "You were with us the whole time!"

"Cronus does not care to tell the truth," Dynam replied. "He is fighting a war and will use every advantage."

The crowd gave us a wide berth this time

around as opposed to last time where they wouldn't get out of our faces. The guards on the walls were on high alert which no doubt influenced the people's behavior.

"I would never want to live here," I muttered to Rhea.

She nodded her head in agreement.

"So many people begging just to get by. I much prefer the fresh air of the forest," she said.

As Harthor led us towards Bevan's home, I could feel the eyes of the crowd on me. They had probably heard about the death of my father. Or even more likely they were merely gawking at the sight of the hulking karcharios that traveled with us.

We entered the building where the council assembled and Harthor told us to wait outside until Bevan came for us. I heard arguing coming from inside the room. One voice was clearly Bevan's. The other was significantly deeper. I wondered briefly if it could have been Cronus but it sounded almost non-human. I strained to hear what they were saying but was unable to.

Then suddenly the door flew open and out stormed a large creature that was as tall and nearly as muscular as Dynam. Only this creature was covered in black fur and had two horns protruding from the top of his head. The beast stopped and stared at Dynam for a moment before storming off muttering something unintelligible.

"Was that a minotaur?" Rhea asked nervously.

"It was," Dynam responded equally surprised.

I peered into the room and saw Bevan standing there. I could see his eyes were red and puffy. He too mourned the loss of my father. He noticed me standing in the doorway and motioned for me to come in.

"Who was that and what was he doing here?" I asked looking baffled.

"That was Mugrish," Bevan said with a sigh. "And he is the Minotaur king."

Bevan's frown softened a bit when he saw my confusion.

"Even I have my superiors," Bevan said avoiding going into further detail.

"Why did your guards try to arrest Dynam?" I asked.

Bevan sighed and lost his smile. "The Blood Hawks beat you here, Chimera. Cronus held a meeting yesterday where he told the council some fabrication about how that karcharios is the one who killed your father."

"But I was there when they attacked us. I know he killed my father!" I said raising my voice.

"Cronus was not giving his side of the argument, he was simply telling a story, however untrue," Bevan said. "The council does not care about the rivalry between your two tribes. That minotaur was just here warning me to keep a war from breaking out at all costs."

My heart sank. If the Sylvan families would not

help us then who would?

"Your best bet," Bevan continued, "Is to return to your village and prepare to defend yourselves."

"Cronus took my brother when they attacked my village," I said. "They are holding him hostage."

Bevan looked away and cursed under his breath.

"That complicates things," he said slowly.

I stood there in silence watching Bevan contemplate what to do.

"Call another council meeting," I said.

"I can't," Bevan said. "Most of the council members have already traveled back to their estates, far from the city," Bevan replied.

I shook my head in frustration.

"Is Cronus still here?" I asked.

"Yes they spent the night but Chimera he's just leaving."

Without letting him finish I stormed out of the room and back to my group. They looked at me with hopeful eyes.

"So," Rhea said, "Will he help us get Anthos back?"

I only shook my head and kept walking. Without asking any more questions my tribesmen continued following me. I walked at a brisk pace back through the streets of Sylvannor towards the gate. When I got to the top of a hill I saw exactly what I wanted to see.

Just inside the entrance to the city were a group of Blood Hawks packing their things and preparing to leave. In the center of the group was a fully armored Cronus. None of them had spotted me. I marched down the road toward them not exactly knowing what I was going to do when I got there.

When I got closer Cronus turned and saw me. A smile grew across his face as he recognized me and he beckoned for his men. The other Blood Hawks drew their swords and formed a line in front of Cronus. I weighed the odds in my head. There were ten Blood Hawks guarding the man who murdered my father. It was an improbable, no, an impossible victory but at least I would die trying to avenge his death.

I unsheathed my own ironwood blade and prepared to charge into battle when I felt Rhea grab my arm and try to hold me back. I took a deep breath and hesitated. Behind me, Dynam and the rest of the hunters readied for a battle. Bevan pushed his way through the crowd until he reached my side.

"Chimera, fighting him now will doom your people who are so desperate for a leader," he said out of breath.

Cronus stepped out in front of his men and stared at me, looking almost amused. The crowd parted when they saw the two of us confronting one another. No one wanted to be caught in the crossfire of two clashing chieftains.

"Chimera, chieftain of the Storm Hunters," Cronus said while mock bowing. "I want to offer my deepest condolences on your father's passing."

"You were the one who murdered him!" I shouted turning red in the face.

Cronus shook his head. "That's not what the council believes."

I was so angry, I just wanted to throw myself at him but Rhea's grip on my arm tightened as if she could sense what I was thinking.

"Don't do anything stupid, Chimera," she said.

The mirth left Cronus' face and he stared daggers at me. He took another step forward, away from the men who protected him and stood proudly in front of me.

"If you really think I killed Andras," he said grimly. "Then avenge his death."

I tightened my grip on my sword and could not hold back any longer. I shook off my sister's grasp and much to the dismay of Bevan I ran towards Cronus with my sword held high above my head. The Blood Hawks who were supposed to protect my enemy remained motionless behind him. I came within reach of my enemy and brought my sword down upon his head.

I was stunned when Cronus caught the wrist that held my sword with one hand and with the other grabbed me by the neck and threw me to the ground. Before I knew what was happening, he landed one forceful punch to the stomach. I gasped for air. I could offer no resistance as the second devastating blow came to the same location as the first.

"I did kill your father," Cronus said viciously in my ear. "And I will kill the rest of your family before I kill you."

The words came with such hatred behind them that I lay completely still and utterly terrified. A single tear rolled down my cheek and I was filled with anger and sadness.

My chest felt like it was going to collapse on itself as I lay there on the ground. I heard loud voices arguing. Cronus was dragged off of me by Bevan and they got into a shouting match with each other. I tried to lift my head off the ground but every movement was painful and I was still struggling to breathe. I opened my mouth to call for help but could not make a noise as I passed out.

* * *

When I woke up I was indoors lying on a bed. Looking around the room I could see that Rhea, Dynam, and Bevan stood around me waiting anxiously for me to awaken. Rhea almost jumped when she saw my eyes open and Dynam gave what seemed to be a relieved expression though I was still learning what his facial expressions looked like. If he had eyebrows then he would be frowning, but not in an angry way.

"Where is Cronus?" I managed to ask.

"He is long gone," Bevan said shaking his

head. "There is no need to worry about him for now."

"We need to get home," I said looking around the room in a panic. "They could attack again at any moment."

Everyone looked at each other without saying anything.

"Didn't anyone hear me?" I shouted.

I knew the odds were slim but perhaps if we left soon we could still save the lives of at least some of my people.

"Can I speak with Chimera alone?" Bevan asked.

The other two only nodded and left quietly.

"Cronus will not risk another attack so soon," Bevan said with a calming voice. "Now, I know you are worried about your brother's safety. But I need to ask a favor of you that your friends have already agreed to."

I frowned, "What would that be?"

"I need you to not retaliate against Cronus."

I was astonished. How could I sit by while my nine-year-old brother was in captivity?

"I give you my word that I can negotiate Anthos release," Bevan said, "But not if you lash out at Cronus like that again."

I took a deep breath and contemplated what Bevan was asking. I hated the thought of doing nothing but the only alternative I could think of was a direct assault which would cost us too many lives.

"How long will it take?" I asked.

"Less than a week."

I hesitated but nodded.

Bevan thanked me and then left. I trusted Bevan, but if he failed to return my brother to me I knew I would not hesitate to declare war on the Blood Hawks. I was going to get my brother back, no matter the cost.

5 - DUST

"So what should I do better next time?" I asked Dynam as we made our way back to the remainder of our village. "He's so much stronger than I am."

"So am I," Dynam said. "You beat me despite that."

I looked at the ground considering what he had just said.

"You played right into his strength," Dynam said. "When you fought me you were agile and used your bow."

I nodded slowly understanding.

"I allowed myself to get too angry."

"And thus, your judgment was clouded," Dynam said smiling.

The rest of the journey home was uneventful other than the brief lightheadedness I felt from the blows I took from Cronus. We arrived at our encampment to see a large group of Storm Hunters trying to salvage food from the half of our camp that was largely in ashes. Some of the people were even burying bodies that had just been found today. I sighed. Even now, days after the attack, my people still grieved over the newly discovered dead.

We walked into camp and almost immediately everyone found work. I, however, was allowed a few moments to visit my father's grave. Due to the state of his body when we found him, Apistos could not wait until our return to bury him. I made my way to the rose oak down by the stream. The scene was not as beautiful as my mother depicted it with her painting. As I approached, I could see the large stone where my grandfather was buried. Now a second stone accompanied it. I thought about saying something but there was no one to hear. No ceremony, just a dead chieftain with no one to mourn him. He never cared much for graveside speeches anyway.

Exhausted and recovering from multiple injuries, I returned to camp only to be put to work helping set up housing for the survivors who lost their homes. It dragged on but the work remained necessary for the rebuilding and defense of our tribe. I couldn't help but think about how much of a waste of time this would be if Cronus decided to wipe us out tomorrow.

Near the end of the day, Apistos and I began working on strengthening the makeshift barricade made from the wreckage that guarded the entrance to the remaining part of our camp. I was able to fill him in on what happened in Sylvannor while we worked. The wind started to pick up and I could tell that it would begin to rain soon. We hurried to get inside before the storm came. The barricade reached a point where it provided just enough cover for us to defend ourselves if need be.

We were heading back inside when another man asked for help lifting one final log to reinforce the barricade. Apistos and I obliged and when I got closer I could see the man was extremely thin.

"Have you eaten recently?" I asked him.

The man sighed, "No sir."

"Go inside and find something to eat," I said. I knew we were low on food but surely we had something for this man. Plus, Terros and his men would hopefully return soon from his hunt with plenty of food for all of us.

"If you don't mind, sir," he said timidly. "I'd rather fortify the encampment before indulging myself. I have a family to protect in there."

"If you insist." I respected the man's devotion to finishing the job.

The man hardly aided in his weakened state but Apistos and I were able to do most of the lifting ourselves.

"Thank you, Chimera," the man said, smiling.

"What's your name," I asked the man.

"Minima," he said enthusiastically. "And I-

He was cut off when out of nowhere an arrow shot out of woods and embedded itself in his skull. I stood there absolutely stunned for a moment staring at the man in front of me who had been alive seconds before.

"Blood Hawks!" Apistos shouted before grabbing my arm and dragging me behind the barricade.

There was a loud commotion as families began to panic at the thought of another attack. A handful of Storm Hunters ran towards the barricade, nocked arrows on their short bows and started scanning the tree line for our attackers.

I took a deep breath and prepared myself for yet another battle. I drew my sword and gripped it tight. The anger from the last few days began to build up again. I assured myself that if need be I would die holding the Blood Hawks at this barricade.

I glanced at the archers peeking over the barricade. It was odd that they hadn't shot yet but perhaps the enemy was concealed in the trees. Another minute passed without any activity outside. I frowned and realized that this wasn't a standard attack.

Much to the dismay of Apistos and all the Storm Hunters, I stepped out from behind the barricade and into the range of whoever shot the arrow. I waited for a moment to see if they would use the opportunity to kill me but nothing happened.

I turned my attention to Minima who now lay dead on the ground. The arrow protruding from his skull had the telltale fletching of the Blood

Hawks, black feathers with red tips. But there was something else tied to the shaft of the arrow. I knelt down and untied the object to examine it.

A small silver coin that on one side depicted a karcharios warrior, and on the other, a magnificent phoenix fanning its wings. My heart sank. I clutched it in my fist as I remembered that I had given the coin to Anthos before I left for Sylvannor with my father. Cronus was sending us a message, and the poor man was just another victim of his cruelty.

I stood up and looked toward where the arrow had come from. I'd never been to the Blood Hawks encampment, but I always knew the general area that it was located. For a moment the thought crossed my mind to go after the shooter and follow him to his tribe's encampment.

I need you to not retaliate against Cronus, Bevan's words echoed through my mind.

But that was before he callously murdered another one of my people.

I turned and walked back into our camp where the Storm Hunters anxiously awaited some news.

"False alarm," I said grimly. "There is no attack."

The panic subsided and many of the warriors let out a sigh of relief. Apistos gave me a confused look and I gestured for him to meet in the makeshift council tent. He only nodded and moved quickly to notify Rhea and Dynam of the impromptu council meeting.

The sky finally opened up and began pouring buckets of rain as evening came upon us. Anyone who had not already returned to their homes did so hurriedly to avoid being totally soaked by the downpour. I moved briskly towards the meeting hut trying to picture what my father would do in this situation. The truth was, I had no idea what he would do. Though the Blood Hawks and Storm Hunters have always been bitter rivals, there had never been a true war between the two tribes.

I arrived at the hut and ducked inside to see I was the first one to arrive. I walked to the center of the room and placed the coin on the small table, lit the candles in the room, and took my seat. Rhea, Apistos, and Dynam all filed in one after another. Dynam and Rhea immediately recognized the coin.

"What is this?" Apistos asked.

"It's the coin Dynam gave me the day we captured him," I said. "Before we left for Sylvannor I gave it to Anthos for safe keeping."

Apistos leaned back in his chair realizing what that meant.

"Cronus is taunting us," I said more forcefully than I meant to. "He knows that we will do anything to get Anthos back."

"What do you want to do about it?" Apistos said. "You said Bevan was handling it."

"We can't wait any longer," Rhea said. "Every night all I can think about is the fact that Anthos is a prisoner in some cage, alone and scared."

I looked at Dynam who maintained a stoic look on his face.

"What do you think, Dynam?" Rhea asked.

Dynam hesitated for a moment. "I believe Cronus wants you to attack him," he said. "The coin is only more proof that he is trying to goad you into a war you cannot win."

Apistos nodded in agreement but Rhea looked disappointed. I pondered his words for a moment.

"We don't have to go to war," I said forming an idea in my mind.

Everyone turned their attention to me waiting expectantly.

"We are the Storm Hunters. We're used to hunting predators," I said looking around the room. "Tonight, we can launch a rescue mission under the cover of darkness. If everything goes right we can get Anthos back without engaging a single Blood Hawk soldier."

Apistos shook his head, "You don't even know the layout of their camp, how do you expect to sneak around without being caught?"

"You do it all the time when you go hunting," Rhea said.

"Yes but we've never hunted people before," Apistos retorted.

I glanced at Dynam to see if he had any input but he did not.

I shook my head defiantly. "No, we're doing

this tonight. I won't let my brother spend another day as the prisoner of that psychopath."

Apistos looked angry but I knew he wouldn't challenge my decision.

"Apistos have the hunters ready by nightfall," I ordered.

He stared at me for a long moment and I wondered if he would voice his disapproval. I raised my eyebrows waiting for his response. An agonizing amount of time passed before he nodded.

"I will meet you at the barricade then," I replied.

He put on his cloak and disappeared into the storm outside.

I turned toward Rhea who seemed hopeful for the first time since our father had died.

"I will get our brother back," I said without a shred of doubt in my mind.

Rhea gave a slight nod and I exited the hut into the downpour with Dynam close behind.

"Let me come with you, Chimera," Dynam said. His low voice barely audible over the wind and rain.

I paused for a moment before shaking my head. "You are too wounded,"

It was hard to say no to the kind beast but I felt I needed to this time.

"Besides," I said. "You're a warrior, and we are not going to war."

With that, I turned and made my way towards

the barricade pulling my already wet cloak over my head. When I arrived, I saw a few hunters already waiting and informed them of the plan. They followed orders diligently. Many of them looked eager for a chance at revenge. Others were more grumpy to be called to duty late at night in the middle of a storm.

We huddled close to the wall which provided a little bit of shelter as more and more hunters trickled in. After what seemed like hours, Apistos showed up and we set out for the Blood Hawks encampment. There were about fifty of us in total. Half the remaining forces of the Storm Hunters. Far more than we needed for a sneak attack but we needed to be prepared for a battle even if it wasn't our goal.

I recognized a young hunter with us named Nameer who actually failed the trials this year but held a bow the same as the rest of us.

"Are you sure you want to come with us?" I asked.

He nodded. "The Blood Hawks killed my father when they attacked. I need to do this."

We traveled a significant distance through our regular hunting grounds, which were now devoid of anything to hunt. It was my first time walking through the graveyard of the forest that once thrived here. Tree stumps were the only remaining scars from the wildfire that devastated the area. We finally came to a neck of the woods I had never been in before. It was good to see green again but this was the Blood Hawks' forest. We sloshed through the muddy paths and used our swords to cut away some of the brush. I wondered how Cronus and his people got to our camp with all the obstacles that we were facing. The forest was so dense clearly no one had traversed this path in the many years since he left the Storm Hunters. The rain began to slow and the ground turned from dirt to rock as we continued moving towards the Blood Hawks camp being much more conscious now of how much noise we made. I had no idea how far out they would patrol but we knew we could run into guards at any minute.

In the distance, I heard faint voices. I held up my hand and the hunters froze behind me. Through the remaining trees and bushes, I could see two warriors standing guard just outside what appeared to be the entrance to the camp. I could see that there was a thick wall of bushes and vines that would make that entrance the only quiet way to get in.

I gestured to Apistos who approached silently. We both nocked arrows on our short bows and seconds later the two sentries were lifeless on the ground. We darted toward the entrance followed closely by the rest of the hunters.

"We'll split up," I whispered to Apistos. "You and Nameer take five hunters to the south side and I'll take five more north."

Apistos nodded. "How will I know if you've

found Anthos?"

I thought for a moment.

"We go in for an hour and if we don't find him by then..." I trailed off.

Apistos understanding, only nodded before going to search his half of the camp. As I moved across the camp I could see it shared a similar grid layout as ours, though they had small stone buildings instead of straw huts. My group of hunters followed me but stayed spread out to avoid detection. I passed barrels and barrels of dragon dust and was surprised that they would be callous enough to keep it in the open. And even more shocked at the extreme wealth they had of it. How did they come by it all? Cronus was stockpiling for more than a war against the Storm Hunters as there was enough here to obliterate the minotaurs.

I dashed across another pathway and halfway across noticed a guard coming right toward me.

"Hey!" The guard shouted as he saw me.

I quickly ran across the path and slid through the mud to hide behind a building. I could hear the obnoxiously loud snoring of someone inside and was relieved when they didn't wake up. I calmly removed my sword from its sheath and waited for the guard to get to the building I was hiding behind. I would have to make sure he stayed quiet.

I could hear his boots sloshing in the mud and I readied myself to attack when an arrow flew from the direction I had come from and landed in the neck of the heavily armored guard. The guard's body landed hard with a splash in the mud. I turned to see that another one of the hunters that had shot the arrow. I nodded toward him in thanks before I realized that it had become quieter all of a sudden. The snoring had stopped.

I listened very carefully and inside the tent, I could hear the man unsheathing his broadsword though only faintly. I held my breath and peeked around the corner to see the man staring at the body of the guard who had just been shot. Panicked and unable to think of anything better to do, I ran toward him and plunged my sword into his back.

The blow was so unexpected to the unarmored man and the ironwood cut through him so cleanly that he didn't make a sound before joining his friend on the ground. I cursed under my breath. Already we had been forced to kill far more than I had hoped and Cronus would be sure to retaliate. As long as I got my brother I would be willing to abandon our camp and move my people as far as I needed. I still grimaced as I moved past the two bodies. I hoped I would never get used to killing but knew I was already becoming desensitized to it.

I quickly moved both bodies inside the building so they wouldn't be discovered by any other guards before putting my head down and continuing to search the camp for cages or any sign of where they might be keeping my brother. I spent what seemed like a lifetime searching before I finally saw at the end of a long line of buildings a small cage that had a person in it.

I ran towards the cage recklessly to try and identify the prisoner. As I got closer I could tell that it was a younger boy who had his back turned to me.

"Anthos?" I whispered but the boy did not move.

I continued to approach the boy until I was just outside the cage.

"Anthos!" I whispered more urgently while trying to break the lock with my sword.

As soon as I got the cage door open I reached in and put a hand on Anthos' shoulder. I was immediately taken aback when I felt how soft it was. I grabbed the boy's shoulder and turned him around to see that it was not a boy after all, but Anthos' clothing stuffed with straw. I felt sick to my stomach as I sat there on my knees in the mud staring at this eerie doll.

I wiped the rain and sweat from my face before holding my head in my hands. All this searching and I still had no leads. Not only that, but Cronus knew my every move. I closed my eyes briefly and realized how truly fatigued I was.

I stood up and tried to remember how Anthos must be feeling. I couldn't possibly be as tired or scared as he was right now. I turned around to see that the other hunters had grouped together hoping that we had found him. I shook my head and signaled for them to keep looking.

I searched the camp and tried to think of the places I hadn't been yet. I was taken aback, however, when the sound of an explosion pierced my ears and I could see a cloud of fire rise into the sky on Apistos' side of the camp. The very ground seemed to shake from the force of the detonation.

I did not know what could have caused the blast but our search for Anthos was over. I quickly ordered the small group of hunters to retreat toward the entrance and they did not hesitate. The whole camp would be alerted by the explosion so I would have to hope Apistos found him.

We sprinted down the muddy path cutting down groggy Blood Hawks who were just catching their bearings in the midst of the midnight raid. A few guards tried to stop us, but on their own they were no match. We came to the center of the explosion and immediately could see that skeletons littered the scorched ground, their flesh melted away instantly from the sheer heat. The bodies were unidentifiable and I worried that more than a few of them may, in fact, be Storm Hunters. Surely Apistos would have gotten away.

Smoke rose high into the air from the fires that had been started on the straw roofs. The inferno was weakened by the rain but still managed to level many of the Blood Hawk structures before being snuffed out. Apistos and his group of hunters were nowhere to be found so we continued toward the entrance to escape.

When we got closer to the entrance I heard screams and the telltale clashing of swords. I drew my own blade and ran toward the commotion without worrying about my own safety. The entryway came into view and I stopped short. The forty hunters we left at the entrance were being attacked from both sides by Blood Hawk warriors. And Apistos was in the middle of it all.

The Blood Hawks had cut off our escape masterfully by hiding a group of their warriors outside the walls in the forest. Apistos was trying to punch through but he was losing too many men too quickly. I scanned the battlefield for Anthos but he was nowhere to be found. Cronus was in the center of the action cutting down hunters left and right. I squinted through the smoke and rain and I could see that Cronus was wielding a long ironwood sword, the very same sword that Bevan had given to my father.

I could feel anger swelling in my chest as I saw my father's blade being used to murder his own people. I gripped my own sword tightly and took a deep breath before charging towards Cronus. One Blood Hawk tried to stop me but I swiftly sidestepped his attack and kept running toward my target.

Cronus had just disarmed another hunter and was about to bring his sword crashing down upon him when, remembering Dynam's advice, I deftly removed my bow from my back and shot an arrow into his shoulder. Cronus roared in pain and turned to face me, his eyes filled with rage. I wondered if he would address me or try to taunt me some more but he did not, he was too full of bloodlust for that.

He charged at me and I raised my sword to meet him. I would avenge my father's death or die trying. It was at this moment that Apistos, summoning all his bravery, threw himself at Cronus tackling him to the ground. I stood still for a moment before running to help Apistos to his feet. Before Cronus could catch his bearings we both leapt into the fray to break through the ranks of Blood Hawks who trapped us here.

Apistos and I stood and fought beside each other cutting down foe after foe. I winced every time a movement reopened the wound in my stomach but we had nearly broken through the enemy's blockade. I turned to look behind me for a moment. We had lost many, but hopefully we still had the numbers to push through.

Behind us, standing far from the fighting, was Cronus who stood tall with my arrow still protruding from his shoulder. I frowned. Surely he would be in the center of the action despite his wound. He made eye contact with me and I froze, an eerie smile beginning to form on his face.

I resolved myself to escape as quickly as possible and leave whatever sick plan Cronus had for us behind when I saw two Blood Hawk soldiers carrying a large barrel to the battlefield. I narrowed my eyes trying to decipher what they could be planning. When they rolled the barrel towards us my eyes widened with horror and I knew instantly what they were planning.

"Dragon dust!" I shouted trying to warn as many hunters as I could.

Storm Hunters and Blood Hawks alike began to scramble but it was too late. I looked at Cronus again, who was now aiming his bow towards the barrel. He released his projectile and the flaming arrow shot toward its target at an alarming rate. I had only a fraction of a second to leap away from the barrel before the arrow ignited it.

The next thing I knew I was lifted off my feet and thrown by a wave of fire. I flew through the air all the while feeling the blistering heat on my back. My screams were quickly silenced when I hit the ground hard. I landed in the woods just outside the Blood Hawks encampment face first in a small puddle of muddy water. The world had gone silent, aside from ringing in my ears, as I lay in the wet dirt completely numb to my surroundings.

It took a great deal of strength to roll onto my side and I felt a searing pain in my back. I knew immediately that I had sustained severe burns. I spit out blood and dirt and tried to figure out where I was. As sound returned I could hear nothing but screams of agony as Storm Hunters and Blood Hawks alike burned alive. I painfully lifted myself to my feet and as my vision cleared I could see that I had been thrown a considerable distance from the battlefield.

I looked back toward the encampment to see Cronus and a small group of Blood Hawk warriors march onto the battlefield to execute any wounded or dying Storm Hunters. They hadn't seen me yet so I took the time to scan the edge of the woods for Apistos or any other hunters who were too wounded to escape on their own. There were none. I leaned against a tree and looked again just to see Cronus put my father's blade through the chest of Nameer who was begging for his life. I gritted my teeth feeling helpless but I needed to do something. I let out a pathetic yelp trying to draw attention away from the defenseless but my cries went unnoticed among the screams of the dying.

I looked again but there was no one who could be saved. I clenched my fist and began to stumble through the dense forest once again toward our camp. Physically I was in agony from the burns, but the emotional pain was far worse. I was returning as the leader of a rescue mission with no survivors. Anthos either remained a prisoner or Apistos had found him and he had been killed with the rest of my men. I didn't even want to consider that possibility. For now, I just desperately needed to get home.

I traveled far slower on the way home due to my injuries and when I finally did arrive back at the village it was nearly the dawn of a new day. I approached our makeshift barricade and the guards let me in, shocked at the shape I was in. They helped me to the medical station where I saw two other hunters were also being treated for burns. They must have also been thrown far enough by the explosion to escape.

I didn't say a word as our healers tended to my wounds as best as they could. When morning came I saw Rhea, her face pale.

"Did you find him?" she asked.

I felt my face grow red with the shame of failing to deliver on my promise. I only shook my head and it devastated her. She sat down beside me and we both stared at the ground for several minutes.

"What about Apistos?" she asked but without much hope.

I hesitated before speaking.

"Most likely dead," my voice cracked with the words and I could not hold back the tears any longer.

Rhea gasped. How could Apistos, the boy I grew up with, be dead?

There was another long silence.

"Cronus, he knows our next move before we

do," I said shaking our head.

"This isn't your fault," Rhea said gently.

Her words were comforting but I couldn't shake the immense guilt I was feeling. I couldn't run away with my people until I got my brother back, but was it right to endanger my people for my own personal reasons?

"Chimera!"

Someone screeched my name outside the hut in a horrifying scratchy voice. I rose hesitantly and exited the hut followed by Rhea. A group of people had gathered around after hearing the chilling scream. I walked towards the entrance of the camp and standing in front of me was the most sickening thing I had ever seen.

Standing in front of me was a man, but from head to toe, his body and remaining clothes were covered in burns. His flesh had been charred and burnt in the most horrendous way. Where he walked he left a trail of ash and blood. I looked closer at the man's face and I grew sick as I realized who he was. Despite the burnt and scarred flesh, I could tell that this nightmarish creature was in fact, Apistos.

My jaw dropped at this realization I stood there like a fool gawking at the mutilated man. Apistos began to limp toward me with fire in his eyes. I remained still, petrified at the sight of the creature in front of me. He continued to come closer. When he was almost upon me he swung his fist at me wildly and I narrowly ducked the weak attempt at a punch. I blinked rapidly as the monstrosity came towards me again. A few hunters stepped forward to interfere but I told them to stop and let me handle it.

"Apistos, what are you doing?" I asked out of breath.

He did not answer and instead tackled me to the ground. He wrapped his charred hands around my neck and began to choke me as hard as he could. I desperately gasped for air while trying to push him off of me with my own hands. My vision had begun to cloud and I was quickly losing consciousness.

It was then that I felt Apistos being pulled off of me and I looked up to see Dynam. He dragged Apistos away as I got back on my feet coughing.

"Take him to the medical station," I said catching my breath. "Treat his wounds but keep a close eye on him."

It had been a horrific night and I hoped that fact, combined with the injuries, had only temporarily sent Apistos over the edge. We were at war now, and I would need all the help I could get.

"You killed them!" Apistos screamed in the same scratchy voice as before. "You killed them all!"

6 - CURSED

It had been two days since our failed rescue attempt. We had not heard anything from the Blood Hawks or the Sylvan families regarding the ramifications of our attack. Apistos was unconscious for most of this time but our healers remained certain that he would survive. I wanted to talk to him but in the few minutes he was conscious he didn't have the energy to speak. I figured he blamed me for the massacre of our people and I couldn't help but agree with him. The lives of many brave hunters had been tossed aside in a failed attempt to save my brother.

Rhea hadn't slept in the last few days trying to keep Apistos alive. I felt guilty going to sleep myself though I knew there was nothing I could do to help her. Besides, sleep was hardly a refuge. In the few hours of sleep, I did get all I could see were the faces of my father and Anthos. In my nightmares, Cronus and more recently the charred face of Apistos haunted me.

The last few days were brutally long. Between worrying about my brother and the death of my father, I had become a shell of the person I was even a week ago. Rhea remained strong and tried to comfort me but I had selfishly pushed her away. Even Dynam with all his wisdom could offer no words to wipe away the pain of the past week.

Now, I sat at the top of a hill overlooking our encampment. The sun was beginning to show over the horizon. Over half of the usually bustling encampment was in ashes and only a handful of our soldiers remained alive. If Cronus wanted to he could wipe us out easily. I had contemplated going to the Sylvan council again for aid but if they did not help us before then they certainly wouldn't after we had attacked the Blood Hawks.

I traced the edge of the coin Dynam gave me with my thumb as I watched the sunrise. The coin that in many places would be considered a relic now served to be my only reminder of Anthos. I looked down at the image of the phoenix on the coin and rolled up my sleeve to view the glowing orange scar that cut across my forearm. I placed the coin on top of the scar almost expecting it to somehow reveal its secrets.

I had received the scar on my very first hunting trip with my father when I was just a boy. I remember how shocked I felt when that elegant creature flew towards me with such fury and the burning sensation I felt when the bird on fire scarred me. My father dedicated a great deal of time to researching the phoenix scar but he never told me why. He only ever said to keep it a secret from strangers and that he would explain it to me when I was older. I had long known that it wasn't natural. The glow intensified randomly and it was hot to the touch. I was starting to believe that the scar was nothing more than a bad luck charm. Perhaps I had been cursed to this life from my childhood.

I could see Rhea beginning the short climb from the bottom of the hill. When she reached the top she sat down in the grass next to me and we watched the sun come over the horizon together. Neither of us spoke as the stunning sunrise unfolded. Down below I could that see the rest of the tribe was slowly coming to life as daylight shined down upon them.

"Apistos wants to talk to you," Rhea said softly.

I stared vacantly into the distance, unmoving.

"Is he stable?" I asked.

"He has full use of his arms and legs and should be able to walk although his body and face are horrifically scarred. He was extremely lucky to have mostly burned his face and chest, and not as severely as we first thought. I am fairly confident he just may survive."

She sighed and angrily picked a handful of grass.

"Mentally I don't know," she said slowly. "All he has said since he woke up is that he wants to talk to you. But Chimera, he attacked you!"

"And he would be a fool to try again," I said.

I remained motionless for a moment before shoving the coin in my pocket, rolling down my sleeve and standing up. I began walking down the hill toward camp.

As I walked, I noticed the morning dew in the grass. I noticed the cool breeze brush against my face and I could hear its movement in the trees. But most of all I noticed my tribesmen hurrying about their daily jobs. I discovered the beauty in watching Dynam help a wounded man walk to his home.

I couldn't help but glance, however, at the half of the camp that was in ashes. I closed my eyes and focused back on the beauty that I took for granted every day of my life and I felt an overwhelming desire to protect it from harm.

I felt a lump in my throat as I came to the medical tent. I had experienced torturous nightmares about my childhood friend for the past two nights. The image of his scorched face was burned into my mind and I couldn't forget the hatred in his eyes.

I mustered the courage and ducked into the tent. Lying on the bed in the middle of the room was Apistos covered in wet rags and healing herbs. When I entered the tent the doctors and healers tending to him left us to talk in private. I noticed in the corner a bucket of burnt pieces of skin that made me gag.

When we were alone, Apistos sat up slowly and leaned forward on the edge of the bed with his back toward me letting the rags fall to the floor. Since he was not wearing his tunic, I could see his back wasn't burned badly at all. Though I did notice his normally long light brown hair was only represented by a few scorched strands.

I cleared my throat awkwardly and I wanted to say something but there were no words appropriate for the situation.

"At a loss for words?" Apistos asked still facing away from me. His voice was deeper and more gravely than usual.

"N-no," I stammered.

Apistos stood and turned to face me revealing the burns that covered his entire face and neck. They were not as bad as they had been two days ago but remained far from a pretty sight. He walked towards me until he was only a few feet in front of me. I stood there unable to look away, yet wanting nothing more. A single tear rolled down my cheek as I looked at my best friend and could see nothing but a monster.

"I wanted to let you know that this war you're fighting is a lost cause."

He turned and walked toward the table to put a shirt on. He winced as the soft fabric scratched against his scorched skin.

"Even if the Sylvan council was ever to get involved it would be on the side of the Blood Hawks due to that stunt you pulled a few nights ago," he continued.

Apistos put on a hooded cloak and looked me in the eyes again.

"And any day now Cronus could attack us with only a fraction of his troops and wipe us off the map."

"What are you doing?" I asked, fidgeting.

He pulled the hood over his head and placed a hand on my shoulder.

"Chimera you are like a brother to me," he said. "But I do not plan on dying in glorious battle. I'm getting out of here before Cronus destroys me along with you."

"You're running?" I asked incredulously.

"I'll find work in the great desert," he said. "I would advise that you get your family and do the same."

"Apistos, the great desert is filled with criminals."

Apistos shook his head.

"The great desert is filled with opportunities," he said smiling.

I stood there looking at my friend, astonished that he was abandoning us, before speaking.

"Apistos, I messed up," I said stepping to block the entrance. "I cost us the lives of good men and I nearly cost you yours. But I can't let you abandon us now when I need you the most."

"I saved more lives than you can count the day we were first attacked," Apistos shouted back pointing a finger in my face, "Lives that you threw away in a poorly planned attack on the Blood Hawks."

We stood there staring at each other and I knew it would come to blows if the argument continued.

"Get out of my way," Apistos said in a low voice.

"Apistos please."

"You're not going to kill me, Chimera," he said smugly. "And you don't have the resources to keep me captive forever. Let me go."

I clenched my fist. I was so furious with him but he was right. I stepped to the side and let him through.

"Very well," he said looking away. "This is goodbye then."

He pulled his handkerchief over his face leaving only his eyes exposed and began to walk past me. And without another word, Apistos was gone. I stood there in shock for a moment. I never even dreamed that Apistos could be a deserter. Although if I'm honest, for a fraction of a second, I also thought about how easy it would be to go with him and leave the war behind.

My thoughts were interrupted when Rhea came into the tent. I was tempted to leave. If I could convince Rhea then we could be gone in minutes.

"Where is Apistos going?" she asked.

I waited before responding. "He's running from the fight."

Rhea frowned. "You mean he deserted?"

I nodded.

"I thought about going with him but, I can't just leave my people, Dynam, and most importantly Anthos to be killed by Cronus."

We stood there in silence for a moment.

"Did you see anything while you were in their camp?" Rhea asked desperately. "Anything at all that would help us find Anthos?"

I shook my head without making eye contact. "If I had, I would have told you already."

The tears began to run down her face and I could see that the grief over losing Anthos was taking its toll on her. We hadn't seen our brother in five days and in both our minds the odds of ever seeing him again continued to lessen. Rhea turned away from me and exited the tent in despair.

I tried to imagine the Blood Hawks encampment again to determine if there was anything I might have missed but I already knew it was pointless. Cronus had destroyed my life and the lives of my siblings with just a few strategic attacks.

Somehow, I had to get my brother back to salvage any sort of a normal life. Apistos was right, we would no longer have the support of the Sylvan families and our own military had been decimated. I was desperate. My only option would be to go back to the Blood Hawks camp and negotiate with Cronus, the man who murdered my father.

Perhaps this was what he wanted all along, to make me reckless enough to walk right into his camp alone so he could execute me on the spot. I no longer cared. It seemed to be the only way I could ever see Anthos alive again.

I strapped my ironwood sword to my back, right next to my bow, and I set off. No one took notice as I walked down the path toward the barricade. The guards seemed puzzled when I told them I was going hunting but they weren't going to stop me.

"Chimera!" Dynam's voice came from behind me.

I turned to see the great creature lumbering toward me.

"Where are you going?" he asked.

I sighed before telling him. "I'm going to Cronus to trade my life for my brother's."

"Chimera-" He began to object but I cut him off.

"You can't change my mind on this one, Dynam," I said sternly. "I have nothing to lose and I need Anthos back safely."

Dynam nodded respectfully. "Then let me come with you."

"I don't plan on doing any fighting."

"Let me prove to you that I am more than just a fighter," Dynam said.

I sighed again. "Fine, but don't try to talk me down."

Dynam shook his head, "I won't."

We waited until evening before we traveled the same path as before on our way to the Blood Hawk's encampment. Part of me didn't want Dynam to be there on the chance that they kill us without hesitation. No need to waste another life. On the other hand, it felt good not to be alone.

On the way, we saw the bodies of two Storm Hunters that had suffered severe burns and made it halfway home before succumbing to their wounds. The grisly scene only served to add to my determination. Dynam and I continued to traverse the unfavorable terrain without stopping for a few hours.

When we were within sight of the Blood Hawks encampment it was nearly dark. Dynam and I emerged from the trees to see that a large portion of the natural wall had been blown open by the barrel of dragon dust. The trees closest to the camp had burned to the ground and many others had suffered damage. I could see that there were several guards standing in the entrance.

"Please stay here, Dynam," I whispered. "There is no need for you to go down with me."

Ignoring my plea, Dynam stepped out of the bushes and into the view of the guards. I took a deep breath before following the selfless creature. For a moment, the guards looked shocked at the sight of the large karcharios but they regained their composure.

"Who are you?" asked the tall guard who

seemed to be in charge.

"I am Chimera Storm Hunter and I need to speak with Cronus."

When they heard my tribe name the guards immediately drew their swords and took me into custody. They hesitated, obviously frightened, but did the same to Dynam. They marched us through their camp with swords at our backs like they had done some great deed in capturing us. I could see that the rebuilding hadn't even started yet. It seemed like all they had done to clean up after the battle was to get rid of the bodies. I could still see the black dirt where the massive explosion had originated from. Blood Hawk warriors lined up on either side of the path and began chanting in a language I did not understand.

"Do you know what they're saying?" I asked Dynam.

"They are speaking the language of my people," he replied, "back when we ruled all of Aragath."

I could hear the deep, true anger in Dynam's voice for the first time since I met him.

"What are they chanting?"

"Son of the Traitor," Dynam grimaced as he said it.

I held my head high in defiance at the mocking chants. As we got closer, the chant became louder until we came to a large tent and the guards told us to stop. Immediately the chanting stopped and all the Blood Hawks fell to one knee. I turned my eyes towards the tent and waited expectantly.

Emerging from the tent was Cronus who surprisingly still wore the bulky armor of his people. He stood tall outside the tent and looked at me. I knew it must have been a new breastplate because it did not have the mark from where my arrow had pierced him in the battle. I wondered how that wound was affecting him. My father's ironwood sword was strapped around his waist.

A small smile crept across his face when he realized that I had surrendered. The smile turned into a flat out grin when he saw I brought Dynam with me. He was somehow more intimidating than usual in the dim light of the torches.

"Where is my brother?" I asked sharply.

I immediately winced in pain as I felt the guard behind me press the edge of his sword into my back.

"Never address him with such disrespect again!" the guard shouted in my ear.

"Please, Kols!" Cronus said angrily. "It was a fair question."

Cronus motioned for the guards to bring us inside his tent outside earshot of the rest of his tribe. When I ducked inside I realized it was much different than expected. On the floor, I noticed a small wooden sword, but not like the classic sparring swords that we used. This one looked more like a toy.

In the center of the room was a large desk that

Cronus sat behind. Draped over the arm of the chair were towels soaked in blood. Scattered around the room, I could see many of the same herbs and medicines that we used. Perhaps Cronus' wound was worse than I thought.

He turned his attention back to me and the smile returned to his face.

"I've had a change of heart, recently," Cronus said coolly. "I no longer want you dead."

I raised an eyebrow at this.

"Do you expect me to thank you?" I asked sarcastically

I suppose that would be a bit too much to ask for," he said chuckling. "But I do have a more serious request to ask of you."

I decided to hear him out but I was not optimistic.

"Throughout the last week, you have proved on more than one occasion that you are truly a great warrior. I have lost many good men to your blade."

My chest swelled with pride. Sometimes praise feels best when it comes from your enemy.

"As you know, through the recent series of events, the Blood Hawks have gained a significant military advantage over your own tribe and at the time of my choosing, we will wipe you out."

Though the thought was grim, I had prepared myself for this reality over the past few days.

"My offer is simple," Cronus said extending his hand towards me. "I want you to forfeit all your authority and join the Blood Hawks."

My eyes widened at this. I was shocked that he would even consider an offer like this.

"And we would be happy to let the karcharios join, too," he said, grinning. "But that is all. You two will join us and the rest of your tribe will be put to the sword."

I looked at the ground in shame. With my own death imminent, It was impossible not to be tempted by the offer a little bit, but I could never allow myself to do what Apistos did.

I shook my head.

"I can't."

"And why not?" Cronus asked.

I looked back at him.

"I would never be able to live with myself. "

"I see," said Cronus.

I stared at him and he seemed to enjoy leaving me in suspense.

"Well then why don't you tell me the power of the phoenix scar?"

I was shocked. How did he know about that? I glanced at my arm to see if it was visible and as usual it wasn't. Then it hit me like a ton of bricks. Anthos must have revealed it to him during interrogation. Whether or not he was tortured I didn't even want to know. All the while my head was spinning, Cronus seemingly enjoying the turmoil he was putting me through. He motioned to the guards still behind me and they rolled up the sleeve of my left arm to reveal the glowing scar. Cronus stared at it for a long moment absolutely mesmerized by it.

"Where is Anthos?" I asked defiantly.

The smile widened on Cronus' face and he ignored my question.

"What if I told you that my best assassins are making their way to your camp to assassinate your sister right now?"

I could feel my heart beating out of my chest.

"You're bluffing," I said nervously.

Cronus shook his head.

"No," he said. "I am not."

I glanced at Dynam whose eyes were wide.

"If I were you I would not hesitate to go save her," Cronus said.

I took a deep breath and tried to focus on my mission. I had to trust our hunters could hold the assassin's off, but they didn't know they were coming.

"No," I said. "I'm not leaving without Anthos."

Cronus raised his eyebrows. "I will release your brother to you after you return home but on one condition."

I fidgeted nervously while I waited for him to continue. If Cronus was telling the truth, every second the assassins were getting closer to home and I desperately needed to be there.

"The karcharios stays here and takes your brother's place."

I narrowed my eyes at Cronus who did not

waver in his offer. Dynam nodded his head and placed his giant hand gently on my shoulder.

"It's okay," Dynam said. "This is worth it."

I nodded back at him trying to hold back tears.

"Thank you," I whispered.

"Go save your sister," Dynam said.

With that, I left the Blood Hawk's encampment leaving behind Dynam to take Anthos' place as their prisoner. I had no choice but to believe Cronus would keep his promise and release my brother. These thoughts clouded my mind as I sprinted back home in a frantic attempt to save Rhea.

7 - PRISONERS

I raced back to our camp desperately trying to utilize every bit of strength I had left to run faster. I didn't notice the branches that cut my face as I flew through the dense forest. I paid no mind to the body of a fallen Storm Hunter as I sprinted past. I cared about nothing other than getting to Rhea to protect her. I had lost Apistos, my father, and Anthos. I could not lose her.

I was slowed many times by hanging vines and fallen trees that caused me to stumble in the darkness. Determined not to let Cronus have another victory I got back up every time and continued my sprint home.

When I emerged from the forest, I could see our camp and everything seemed normal. I ran to the barricade. The guards immediately let me in and I asked them if they had seen the assassins. They were perplexed and told me they had seen nothing so I hurried past them.

I quickly made my way further into our camp but I was no longer in a complete panic. Either Cronus was bluffing or I had beat the assassins and now I only needed to find Rhea and get her somewhere safe. I hurried down the path asking people where she was and that's when I heard a blood-curdling scream.

I rushed around a corner to see a large group of people gathered in the path. I pushed and shoved my way to the front of the crowd and found that there were three assassins two of which had bows trained on the crowd. The third held a struggling Rhea and had a dagger to her neck. They wore long hooded black cloaks which helped them travel unseen at night and they all covered their faces with layers of cloth. All three were adorned with the black feathers of the Blood Hawks. I clenched my fist, how did they get past our defenses?

I quickly nocked an arrow on my bow and aimed for the one who had Rhea. She looked at me with her eyes darting around looking for a way out but I tried to block my sister out and focus on the assassin. I exhaled slowly and closed one eye looking down the shaft of my arrow at the target. It was a difficult shot but one I was confident I could make.

I hesitated too long. One of the assassins lowered his bow and drew a long sword.

"Don't move!" I shouted at him.

The third assassin still trained his bow at me forcing the standoff. This was clearly not how the assassins planned their attack but with a hostage, they had the upper hand.

It was at this point, that I heard a familiar

battle cry from behind me. The crowd turned to look but I kept my focus on the assassins. I could see, out of the corner of my eye, Terros and about twenty other hunters rush to my side with their bows raised only adding to the stalemate. Relief washed over me. Terros could not have returned from his hunt at a better time. I looked at Rhea who still struggled within the grasp of her captor. She gave me a small nod. I didn't know exactly what she planned but I did my best to ready myself.

Rhea kicked backward at the shin of the assassin who held her and shoved him away. I released my arrow into the distracted assassin and it sunk into his heart. The assassin who aimed at me loosed his arrow which struck my side. Terros' hunters all released their arrows into the assassin who shot me killing him instantly. And finally, the assassin who wielded the sword lunged towards Rhea. I rushed toward her to intercept the blow ignoring the pain in my side.

I lowered my shoulder and rocked the assassin sending him tumbling to the ground and causing him to lose his sword. He nimbly regained his footing and revealed two curved black daggers. We danced for but a moment before I knocked aside his weapons and plunged my sword deep into his chest leaving it there.

I stood and began to feel nauseous. Looking around at the three bodies from yet another attack against my people, I reached and felt the arrow in my side realizing just how much it hurt. I began to stumble before Terros caught me and helped me back to my hut. He let me down onto a cot and I rested.

When I awoke it was light again. Someone had removed the arrow from my side and dressed the wound. It still ached, however, as I tried to stand. I exited the hut and could smell the light rain. I hobbled toward the barricade where I found Terros on watch duty.

"Terros," I said.

He ran toward me. "How are you already walking?"

"I feel, fine actually."

"Chimera you were shot."

"I know. But we need to decide what to do about the Blood Hawks."

"Rhea told me everything. I will speak with you in a few hours to determine our next move," he said shaking his head. "In the meantime, I sent a few men to figure out how those assassins got into our camp unseen. You need to sit down."

I nodded and he returned to the barricade. I turned and limped my way toward the council tent. When I arrived I sat in one of the four chairs and contemplated my situation. As I looked around the room at the other chairs it only provided more motivation. Apistos deserted, Dynam was a prisoner, Rhea nearly assassinated, and it all could be blamed on Cronus.

I slammed my fist on the table as I thought

about the events of the past week. It became so easy to throw the blame on Cronus but I knew that I could have handled every situation better myself. And now I fought not to let my anger decide my actions for me yet again. As if all that wasn't enough Cronus knew about the phoenix scar and wanted me to join him.

I decided I needed to see Rhea and so I left again to go to the medical station. On my way I saw an elderly man I recognized as Paer. He was carrying a bucket of water from the stream back to his home. A job that would usually be taken care of by his grandson, Pervenis.

"Let me help you with that," I said.

"Thank you Chimera," Paer said smiling. He was always an optimist.

"I'm so sorry about your grandson."

Paer shook his head still smiling.

"You can hardly be blamed for the wrongdoings of others. You can only do what you think is right, everytime you are given the opportunity."

We arrived at his hut and he thanked me again.

"Paer," I said before leaving. "I won't let anymore of my people die."

"No," he said shaking his head. "I don't believe you will."

When I got to the medical station I saw Rhea helping with the injured. It was sickening to see the wounds many of our people had. A few were so bad they'd lost limbs. I realized I was one of the lucky ones. She stopped when she saw me and ran to embrace me.

"I'm sorry," I said.

She shook her head. "It's hardly your fault."

We stood there in awkward silence. No words could quite convey the emotions we felt in the past few days. I turned and looked at the wounded. I knew it was at least partially my fault what happened to these people. I had to make it up to them somehow.

"All these people's lives ruined trying to get Anthos back," I said.

"No," Rhea said shaking her head. "Cronus did this to them."

It was then that I saw Terros walking hastily toward me.

"Chimera," he said panting. "A caravan from the Sylvan council has arrived and they are waiting outside the barricade."

I frowned and turned my head.

"Who is leading them?" I asked.

"A man named Bevan Haldreithan," Terros replied.

I rushed outside the hut to see for myself with Rhea not far behind. Sure enough, when I reached the barricade I could see Bevan and a group of Sylvan warriors wielding ironwood spears standing waiting for me. They brought with them a cart that was stocked full of produce.

"Well," Bevan said looking up at me. "Are you going to let us in?"

For a brief moment, I almost smiled again before ordering the barricade to be removed from the path. Our visitors did not hesitate to enter and neither did the Storm Hunters delay to take the food. The Sylvan warriors marched forward in unison alongside the cart before breaking formation and handing out the food they had brought. I stood there in awe watching Bevan and his men give my people the food they so desperately needed. Between this and Terros' hunt, we had food to last us until we could get to that piece of land.

"Chimera," Bevan said waving me over. "I have someone who I think you'll want to see."

I walked towards Bevan, skeptical, but when I saw who he referred to pure joy came over me. In front of me, crossing his arms and looking dejected was my brother, Anthos. Rhea flew past me and embraced him. I ran forward relief washing over me; however, when I really looked at my younger brother I was overcome with sadness.

Anthos was covered in dust and his short hair was matted against his forehead. He wore tattered clothes that were torn in many places. I could see tears rolling down his face and he looked at me with fear in his eyes.

I turned toward Bevan.

"We came across him just a mile down the road," Bevan said softly. "I'm not sure what you did to get him released but it worked."

I gulped. Cronus made good on his word by releasing Anthos, but only at the cost of losing Dynam.

"Chimera," Bevan said walking toward me. "We have a lot to talk about."

I led him and Terros to the council tent. Rhea helped Anthos behind us. I could hear the celebration of my starving people behind me but I knew that was only momentary. Cronus was still out there and he was determined to wipe us out.

We entered the hut and Bevan gave Anthos a piece of bread.

"He hasn't said a word since we found him," Bevan said shaking his head.

I nodded and took a seat next to my brother who appeared emotionless.

"The council was in an uproar after you attacked the Blood Hawks," Bevan said.

"I was only trying to get Anthos back," I replied. "You should know, the Blood Hawks had barrels of dragon dust that they used against my people."

Bevan's face turned pale when he heard this.

"Dragon dust?" he asked again in shock.

I nodded slowly, "Enough to raise an attack against Sylvannor."

Bevan wiped a bead of sweat from his forehead. If Cronus had become a threat to the Sylvan families then what chance did we stand against him? I waited while Bevan stared at the floor still in shock.

"I will inform the council of this," he said slowly. "Anthos…"

Bevan paused while thinking of what exactly he could say that would get the boy to speak.

"When you're comfortable, do you mind telling us where they held you?"

I looked at Anthos who nibbled at the bread before finally speaking timidly.

"In a cave."

It felt so good to hear him speak the three simple words. Bevan sat back in his chair, realization falling over him. Terros perked up.

"When we were searching for how the assassins got into our camp," Terros said, "we found the entrance to a cave that was completely hidden by grass."

"What are the odds that cave leads all the way back to the Blood Hawks encampment?" I asked, frowning.

"It does," Bevan said. "Terros would you mind taking Anthos outside for some fresh air?"

Terros nodded, understanding, and left with Anthos right behind him.

I looked at Bevan wondering how he could be so sure.

"The boy doesn't yet know of his father's death," he said, his eyes falling to the floor. "I can't say I know how to tell him the truth but now is not the time."

I nodded and took the opportunity to fill him in on everything that had happened. Everything about Apistos deserting, Rhea's assassination attempt, and Dynam's sacrifice.

"Why would Cronus want you to join him after killing your father?"

My face grew red. I knew the answer to that but should I tell Bevan? I looked at Rhea who nodded. I sighed hesitantly before realizing there wasn't much of a choice, I would have to trust him.

I rolled up my sleeve slowly to reveal the shining orange scar on my forearm. Bevan's eyes widened and he stared in awe at the unnatural mark. After a moment, Bevan removed the glove from his left hand to show that on the back of it there was an orange shimmering scar that traveled all the way to his wrist.

I gasped when I saw it, "You also have the phoenix scar?"

Bevan nodded.

"I got it many years ago when I was in a battle. The phoenix came out of nowhere and scarred me," he said. "Did your father also have the scar?"

"No," I replied. "But he knew that I had it."

Bevan nodded his head in realization.

"Some time ago, Andras came to me in an attempt to discover the secrets of the scar," Bevan said. "I immediately assumed he had it but now I know that his questions were not for himself, but for you."

I was thrilled to finally find someone who also

knew of the scar.

"What do you know about how it works?" I asked.

Bevan shook his head solemnly. "Very little, I'm afraid. Only that it seems to slow aging."

I frowned, "How old are you?" I asked Bevan, who looked to be no more than ten years older than myself.

"I am entering my 54th year," he said.

I looked at him and shook my head in awe. He was the same age as my father yet appeared to be young enough to be my brother.

"Beyond that," he said. "I have dedicated years of my life to discovering it's secrets and have found nothing."

I looked at the ground, disappointed.

"Do you know anyone else who has it?"

A faint smile came over Bevan's face and he seemed to be reminiscing over something.

"I do," he said. "But I'm sworn to secrecy. I assure you it's no one you know."

I nodded and shuddered. I was beyond excited to finally hear that there were more people like me.

"Now I don't know what power if any, this scar holds," Bevan said covering his hand with the glove again. "But we cannot allow Cronus to discover its secrets."

"Then what's our play?" I asked.

"If I'm right, then this cave system that Terros mentioned leads directly to the Blood Hawks encampment. If this is where your brother was being held then it is more than likely we will find Dynam there as well."

"Then we will go there at once," I said, standing.

Bevan nodded and stood as well. He placed his hand on my shoulder, looked me square in the eyes, and spoke somberly.

"Cronus means to wage war against all of us. He hordes dragon dust, captures a mighty karcharios, and he researches the power of the Phoenix scar. If we do not stop him, it could mean the end for your people and mine."

I gulped and nodded.

"Be ready in one hour," he said.

Bevan marched out of the hut and ordered his men to prepare themselves. I hesitated to leave my people yet again but I knew that it was necessary. I found Terros and told him to stay behind and protect the remaining Storm Hunters.

I found Anthos sitting in the grass not far away and sat beside him.

"I'm sorry I couldn't protect you," I said. "We're going out to get the shark-man back so I wanted to say goodbye."

He didn't react. I handed him the coin that Dynam had given us only a few days ago.

"Hang on to that for me," I said.

I kissed him on the head before standing to leave. I went to find Bevan so we could save Dynam, to whom I owed so much.

8 - MONSTERS

I met up with Bevan and his men before setting out. Terros lead us to the entrance of the cave which was located in behind the village. That explained how Cronus' assassins had infiltrated our camp without anyone noticing. I looked at the cave now which was only a small hole in the ground covered by grass.

"Are you sure this is it?" I asked Terros.

"We searched the area thoroughly," he said. "If they came through a cave, this was it."

With that, I bid Terros farewell and he returned to the barricade to keep watch over the camp. The Sylvan warriors did not hesitate to drop into the cave. After a moment I lowered myself in behind them. The warriors ahead of me held lanterns but it remained very dim. I could see that it was only wide enough for us to go single file and some of the warriors had to duck to avoid the roots that hung from the dirt ceiling.

Bevan dropped in behind me and we began making our way through the cave. I could feel that we were walking on a downward slope and I noticed the ceiling turned to stone. We hiked through the darkness for what seemed like ages before the passage slowly began to open up and Bevan could walk beside me.

"I don't know what kind of opposition we will face," he said. "But be ready for anything,"

I nodded and looked at the warriors in front of me. There were only fifteen of them but they each carried an ironwood spear and had a small shield of the same material on their backs. The perfect combination for holding small passageways. That combined with their elite training from the Sylvan families and these men could probably defend this tunnel against a hundred.

Just when my eyes were beginning to adjust to the darkness, I started to see a faint red glow ahead of us and got the feeling that we were nearing the end. As we got closer, the glow became brighter and sure enough, the cave opened up into a giant cavern. The warriors stepped aside to let Bevan and I see what lie ahead of us.

My jaw dropped and I stared at the vast expanse. Below us, I could see a pit that at the bottom was filled with what I assumed to be molten lava. There were multiple walkways that snaked across the pit and they all led to a platform in the side of the cave on the other side. I had to squint but I thought I could see Dynam tied to a pole on that platform. He was surrounded by the Blood Hawks who appeared to have an entire mining operation underway. Behind them was a shimmering red wall that they were mining. I did not know what they were skimming from the mysterious surface but I knew I wanted to get a closer look.

I was astounded that this massive cavern had been here all the years of my life yet I had never noticed it beneath my feet. I glanced at Bevan who did not seem half as surprised as I was.

"If we do this quickly," he said a bead of sweat running down his forehead. "We can be in and out before anything goes wrong."

"That pathway will keep us concealed for most of the way," I said pointing towards one on the right side. "After that, we'll have to blitz them."

Bevan nodded.

"Chimera, try to avoid any kind of loud noises," Bevan's skin actually looked pale despite the red glow. "You will never understand the fragility of the situation we are about to enter."

I frowned and looked at him but knew that he wasn't about to tell me what made the situation so precarious. I glanced around briefly at the other Sylvan warriors who surprisingly didn't seem to know what Bevan referred to either though they remained unshaken.

We returned to single file as we traversed the narrow walkway that had been carved into the side of the rock wall. At times we had to duck to stay out of sight of the Blood Hawks on the other side of the pit. We moved swiftly and expertly across the precarious cavern in no time at all.

I could see in front of us a small side cave in the wall. When we passed it I froze thinking I saw a Blood Hawk looking right at us but, in reality, it was only an empty suit of armor. I took a closer look at the red tipped black feathers that adorned it and realized that I was looking at the armor normally worn by Cronus. I looked at the Sylvan warriors ahead of me who continued forward. I was about to follow them when something caught my eye. Next to the suit of armor was my father's ironwood sword, gifted to him by Bevan.

I stepped into the cave and moved to take back my father's elegant weapon when I suddenly felt something smash into the side of my head and I fell to the floor. I tried to get back to my feet but failed. My vision clouded. I collapsed onto my back drifting into unconsciousness when I faintly saw that it was none other than Cronus who hit me with a rock. His ominous smile was the last thing I saw before I passed out.

* * *

When I regained consciousness, I found myself on the platform that we had been trying to reach my arms tied behind a pole. I looked up to see that I was now surrounded by Blood Hawks. To my right stood Dynam also tied to a pole. It didn't look like he had been tortured but his expression told me that he was saddened to see I got myself caught trying to rescue him.

"Chimera," he whispered still looking straight ahead. "Did Cronus release Anthos?"

"Yes," I said.

Dried blood kept me from seeing out of my left eye and the massive headache I had told me that the hit I took from Cronus did more damage than I thought. I could see in front of me a crack that led to the surface with molten lava slowly seeping out of it.

That must've been what caused the wildfires! And that crack must've been opened up when the earthquake happened. So that really was the cause of the famine. Really of the whole situation in which we found ourselves.

I craned my neck around to see if I could catch a glimpse of the shimmering red wall that I saw earlier but I could not get myself turned around enough to see. Unfortunately, my moving around alerted the Blood Hawks that I was awake.

"Chimera Storm Hunter," I heard the voice of Cronus as he stepped out in front of me again wearing his armor. He now had both my father's and my own ironwood swords. He clearly enjoyed taunting me.

"Tell me," he continued. "I never did hear what happened to your sister."

I spit at his feet in some feeble act of defiance and he let out a laugh.

"Nothing good I presume," he said.

He tilted his head and looked around the

cavern toward where I came from.

"So, why did you come here in full confidence that you could rescue your Karcharios friend by yourself?"

He turned back to me and I raised my eyebrows. He took notice laughing again.

"So you're not here by yourself after all."

I kicked myself. I had unintentionally given away Bevan and his men.

"I would have thought that all your warriors had been wiped out when you so callously attacked my camp," Cronus said, gesturing with my father's sword towards the rest of the cavern. "But don't worry. Whatever Storm Hunters you have waiting in this cavern will be swiftly put to the sword when they try to rescue you."

I felt a glimmer of hope. Cronus still thought that I had come with Storm Hunters. As much as I believed in my own men, the Sylvan warriors had far superior training and much more dangerous weapons. They had a good chance to catch Cronus off guard if they executed their plan correctly.

Cronus decided he'd had enough fun for now and went back about his business. I looked at Dynam whose eyes were shut.

"Dynam!" I whispered. "Be ready for a fight."

The great Karcharios nodded and straightened himself. His eyes remained closed however and he seemed to be almost meditating. I looked around and spotted my bow leaning against a barrel full of dragon dust. Looking around, I realized that just like everywhere else the Blood Hawks owned, this place had many barrels of dragon dust scattered about.

I tried to take note of all their locations in case they needed to be used in the battle ahead. It was difficult to count but there may have been nearly forty Blood Hawk warriors in view. I began working on the rope that bound my hands behind the pole and realized whoever had tied my hands had done a poor job.

Cronus finished whatever he was doing behind me and came back into sight to continue toying with us.

"You may be wondering why you are not dead yet," he said, addressing both Dynam and me. "That is because my offer from before still stands. I am giving you the opportunity to jump ship before I wipe the Storm Hunters off the map."

Dynam and I remained quiet in our resolve. Something told me Cronus knew deep down that we would never accept his offer after everything he had done. But that didn't stop him from trying.

"This is your final chance," Cronus said stepping toward me while pressing my own sword against my neck.

"Don't!" Dynam shouted at Cronus.

Cronus whirled around and slashed Dynam in the arm with the other blade. Dynam roared out in pain. The wound wasn't lethal but was enough to cause bleeding. Cronus and Dynam were in a stare down. Dynam attempted to stifle his grimace but failed.

Out of the corner of my eye, I saw one of the Sylvan warriors dart past an opening. I frantically tried to untie myself. Cronus turned his attention to me and right as he did, I loosened the knots just enough to slip my hands out. I slapped my sword out of his hand. Cronus was surprised I and couldn't react quickly enough. I shoved him away from me and retrieved my blade from the ground. As I did this, the Sylvan warriors let out a cry and charged onto the platform led by Bevan who wielded twin ironwood blades.

Immediately after retrieving my own blade, I turned and cut Dynam free from his bonds. He let out a roar that terrified all the nearest Blood Hawks. Cronus rolled to his feet and managed to get out of the way of the Sylvan warriors who fought their way to Dynam and me. When we all gathered together, we circled up to find that we were surrounded. Not one Sylvan warrior had fallen, yet but in turn, only a few Blood Hawks had been slain. Despite the Sylvan warriors' superior training, the Blood Hawks were no pushovers and they had the numbers advantage.

Bevan quickly barked out orders to fight around Dynam as his size provided a beacon for us to rally around. The Blood Hawks charged in and many were cut down quickly failing to penetrate the shield wall. The sounds of iron blades clashing against our wooden ones echoed throughout the cavern. I looked up to see a few archers release their arrows toward us. One of the arrows landed in Dynam's back with a thud and, though not killing him, the beast was clearly in extreme pain. He wheezed as he grabbed another Blood Hawk and shoved him into the pit where he fell to an agonizing demise.

We continued to push the Blood Hawks back and I had my eyes set on Cronus whose eyes darted around. His men fell left and right. I parried a blow from one foe before stabbing my blade into the gut of another. It was then that another explosion rocked the cave. I fell on my back not far from the edge of the cavern.

I stood to see that the Blood Hawks were scattered. Many tried to help the wounded ones but for those that were burning nothing could be done as their suits of armor had melted into them. Many of the Sylvan warriors however also suffered great injury. I looked up to see that Cronus, once again, had killed both his men and ours with a barrel of dragon dust.

Cronus met my gaze before turning and running towards the exit that led to their camp. His surviving men followed him. I frowned. They still had the numbers. Why were they running?

My confusion grew when the ground continued to shake long after the explosion had dissipated. It was the kind of deep-rooted shake that felt like it was coming from far below the surface. I began to fear another earthquake and how much more violent it would be if we were caught underground.

"Chimera!" Bevan shouted in a panic. "Run!"

I followed him and Dynam back down the path we came from. Rocks fell from the ceiling all around us as the shaking grew more violent. I turned, curious as to what could be causing this quake. I could see that the tremors seemed to originate from the red shimmering wall. Bevan and Dynam did not stop fleeing as I stared in wonder. Then, the entire red wall disappeared leaving only a dark opening where before an entire wall of the cavern had been.

The shaking stopped and things grew eerily quiet. I looked around the silent cave and heard only a mysterious wind coming from somewhere. Then suddenly, the single largest creature I had ever seen burst through the opening smashing the platform where we had just fought and let out an ear-splitting roar. The red, shining beast had its four feet planted in the bottom of the pit, unharmed by the lava, yet its head still scraped across the ceiling. On its back were two massive wings that it flapped causing violent winds to rip through the cave almost knocking me off my feet. When the monster stood, a cloud of thin red dust fell from its scales. The gigantic talons and its crushing jaws petrified me. The creature was something only my darkest dreams could have imagined. It was something described in the tales the elders told our children. The stories were told as pure fiction, but the name these creatures shared was always the same. The red shimmering wall was not a wall, but a dragon.

I stopped gawking and sprinted back across the pathway trying desperately to escape before the creature noticed me. I was too late, however, and the dragon turned its head towards me and released a scorching wave of fire from its mouth.

I narrowly avoided the blast by diving into the tunnel we came from and where Bevan, and two other warriors, planted themselves bravely holding their ironwood shields to block the deadly dragon's breath. I could feel the intense heat on my face and Bevan let out a shout as the inferno began to melt the shield. He dropped it immediately when the flames caused his hands to redden. The other warriors were in the same condition.

We continued to run deeper into the tunnel fleeing from an enemy that seemed impossible to fight. I could hear the dragon's roars echo as he thrashed about in the cavern behind us trying to claw his way out through the ceiling, causing another earthquake. The smell of sulfur filled the air and choked my lungs.

We could only run for so long before Dynam needed to rest. Bevan hesitated but allowed us a moment. I sat down and realized how much I was sweating, not only from the heat but from the sheer intensity of what I had just witnessed. I looked at Bevan who did not return eye contact.

"What has a dragon been doing underneath us this whole time?" I asked, incredulously.

Bevan sighed and waited a long time before answering. "Many years ago, before I was even born, the Sylvan families were attacked by this dragon. The stories vary but somehow through their weapons or their magic my ancestors were able to lure the beast far underground and put it to sleep."

I looked toward Dynam who seemed more angry than confused.

"We knew that eventually the beast would be awakened so we sealed off the tunnels and prepared ourselves for another fight. I never expected that one of the tribes we were meant to protect would be the ones to awaken it."

I leaned back against the wall still taking it all in. A dragon was on the loose in Aragath. The thought was so ridiculous, it almost made me laugh aside from the fact that it meant a lot of people were going to die.

"My people called him Vulcanor," Dynam said solemnly. "And he is the king of all dragons. Though my people were told the beast had been killed."

Bevan sighed. "The Sylvan families knew the dragon's scales could be mined to produce the valuable substance called dragon dust. Their greed prevented them from killing the beast."

"That dragon caused the earthquake, which caused the famine, which caused this terrible war," I yelled at him.

"I understand your anger. Keeping the dragon a secret was the greatest sin of my ancestors," Bevan said. "Perhaps I should have warned you but I didn't want word to get out. It would only cause more greedy people to attempt to mine it.

We sat there in silence for a time and I started to wonder what Cronus had unleashed on the world, intentionally or otherwise. When Dynam was well rested, we finished the underground journey back to our camp. I exited the cave to see there was now a thin layer of snow and temperatures had dropped again. The weather simply refused to conform to our seasons. I could see Terros walking toward me and he had a worried expression on his face.

"Chimera, it's a good thing you're back."

He looked disappointed to see there were less of us returning but shook it off and pointed toward something on the horizon. I looked and saw a towering plume of black smoke rising slowly towards the sun. A fire raged at the Blood Hawks encampment.

I looked at Bevan who pursed his lips. "All the dragon dust they were hoarding, combined with dragon fire..." he trailed off but I got the idea.

The Blood Hawks would be destroyed by Vulcanor's flames without walls to hide behind.

"Dragon fire?" Terros tilted his head.

"Yes from a dragon. A very large and angry one too. There is no time to explain further," Bevan said. "Time is our most valuable resource. Do you have a horse I can borrow?"

"Sure," I stammered. "But they are plow horses never trained for riders."

Bevan shook his head. "It doesn't matter. Chimera, I hate leaving you but I must go to my people and warn them of the demon that comes for us all."

"What are we supposed to do?" I asked.

Bevan paused for a brief moment. "Bring your people to Sylvannor. And not just the warriors. You need to get all your people behind our walls. There, we will have a chance to beat this thing together. Here, you will be slaughtered."

I ordered Terros to begin the evacuation and Dynam to get his wounds fixed up. I led Bevan to the stable where I was surprised when he expertly mounted the horse without even saddling his ride. The horse that bucked every rider who'd ever tried to mount him, was immediately willing to carry Bevan.

"Ride fast," I said, patting the horses back.

"And you use your time wisely," he replied. "For there is precious little of it."

He made a clicking sound and the horse trotted off. I watched him ride for a moment before hurrying to the council hut to pack my things. When I finished, I stepped outside to see that my people had wasted no time in their preparations. An evacuation of this size would have been impossible before the war with Cronus. Ironically, our smaller number actually gave us a chance.

I approached the medical station to see that Rhea was helping Anthos out to one of the wagons. It was then that Terros came up to me walking briskly.

"Chimera, we are ready to move out," he said.

We exited the hut and Terros led us to a large crowd of people with three carts pulled by the fat moulin beasts. I helped Anthos into the wagon with Rhea and we began our journey to Sylvannor. I caught up with Dynam whose wound had been bandaged heavily. He pointed toward the horizon and I looked to see the plume of smoke was no longer black but instead it was white.

"White smoke means the fire has gone out," Dynam said, warily.

I stared at the ominous marker in the sky before turning away and nervously picking up the pace. I knew that if Vulcanor was done with the Blood Hawks he would next come for us.

9 - CHIEFTAINS

Dynam and I led the Storm Hunters down the path to Sylvannor that I was becoming so familiar with. The other remaining warriors spread out along our caravan with Terros bringing up the rear to warn us of danger. We made good time despite having our wounded with us. I breathed hot air on my hands in an attempt to return feeling to them. If we were called to fight I did not want to have numb fingers.

In the ground, I could see the horse prints in the thin snow where Bevan had ridden ahead of us. By now, I hoped he had reached his people and was already preparing a defense. A brief gust came from behind me and I whirled around to see the sky was empty. I was paranoid that every little breeze could be the dragon's wings coming to give us a swift demise. I looked at my people lined up on the path behind me and bit my lip. We weren't moving fast enough.

I put my head down and continued to move. I could hear the faint whispers of my people's gossip behind me and I realized that I probably seemed crazy to them right now. Dynam and I were the only ones who knew about Vulcanor. Bevan was right though, we had no time to lose and if I got them to safety I would explain everything later.

I started to with anger. Anyone whose life the dragon took, their death would lie solely on Cronus' shoulders. He didn't deserve the quick death that Vulcanor had most likely given him.

"Be careful, Chimera," Dynam said noticing my face turning red. "Anger is not your ally,"

I took a deep breath and nodded.

"Have you ever fought a dragon, Dynam?" I asked.

He shook his head. "I have only heard stories about this one."

"You referred to him as the king of all dragons," I said.

Dynam nodded. "There is no doubt he is the fiercest and most aggressive of the dragons. Before my people died out we were told that the beast had been slain. Now I know that we were deceived."

We continued down the path and when we started to approach the city I heard strange noises ahead of us. Dynam, Terros, and I scouted ahead to see what was going on and I hoped that Vulcanor hadn't beaten us. We hid just inside the tree line and had the perfect view of the city.

What I saw was not a dragon, but an army of Blood Hawks outside the city gates. There may have been nearly five hundred of them all chanting and beating on their war drums. Among their ranks were four large armored catapults loaded with barrels of what could only be dragon dust. I craned my neck to see if Cronus was among the ranks but could not see him. There was a possibility he ordered the attack before Vulcanor laid waste to their camp.

Lining the walls of the city were the men of the Sylvan armies all wearing ironwood armor with house sigils on the chest. They also had mounted crossbows the size of catapults. They were loaded with bolts large enough to kill ten men, or a dragon.

"How are we going to get our people inside when the Blood Hawks are blocking the entrance like that?" Dynam asked.

"There's a side gate that we can get our people through quickly but with a group this size we will most likely be spotted," I replied, pointing toward the gate.

"We can buy time," Terros said. "We can take shots at the Blood Hawks from the tree line."

I nodded realizing that this plan would put us in extreme danger but also knowing that it was the only way to get my people to safety. We swiftly retreated and informed the people of the plan. I could see the looks on their faces and knew they were fearful but no one opposed the plan. I gathered every remaining bowman we had and we set out to cause a distraction.

We spread out within the tree line. Terros took

his men further right while I took mine left. Dynam stayed in the middle to deal with any Blood Hawks who charged us. I quietly gave the orders for my men to nock arrows before signaling for my people to make for the gate.

I trained my bow on the first Blood Hawk who noticed my people making a beeline for the gate and released my arrow into neck. A small volley of arrows came out of the trees after that cutting down more Blood Hawks. Our cover was blown but our foes were taking arrows from both sides. The Blood Hawks were scrambling now that they were surrounded and paid no mind to our people running to the gate. It only took one man, however, to restore order to their ranks.

"Take cover behind the catapults! Archers on both sides! Prepare to counterattack!"

I heard his voice and then I saw his face. Cronus was alive. He stood bravely in the open commanding his troops. I went to nock another arrow but fumbled it on my bowstring. By the time I had it on my bow and was ready to fire, Cronus had disappeared behind one of the catapults. I wondered briefly if I'd imagined him but I knew I couldn't have. He was here in this battle and I was determined to find him.

The hunters released another volley of arrows but most of the Blood Hawks had hidden behind cover. As soon as our volley landed I heard the words I most dreaded.

"Charge!"

The Blood Hawks stampeded toward us. They outnumbered us and if they closed range we wouldn't stand a chance. We loosed another volley of arrows but barely made a dent in their frontline. Terros and I both ordered our men to form up as we made our last stand. Dynam bravely took his place in our front line and I stood alongside him. We braced ourselves for battle.

I may have been the first to notice when the winds started to whip the trees back and forth violently but as it grew stronger I actually had to steady myself against one of the trees. The charge of the Blood Hawks came to a halt and I could see the terror in their eyes as they looked to the sky behind me. I followed their gaze and froze as I saw Vulcanor swooping toward us.

The dragon threw his head back and let out a hot stream of fire that incinerated the tops of the trees before making its way to the ground. I threw myself out of the path of the flames and turned around to see the monster's rampage. The inferno cut through the ranks of the Blood Hawks killing many of them and shattering their charge. Multiple large explosions rocked the ground as the flames made contact with the dragon dust barrels.

Vulcanor continued towards the walls of the city. Hundreds of arrows shot from the bows of the Sylvan archers, many hitting their target, but not one penetrated the demon's scales.

Vulcanor took a breath before shooting another ray of fire at the archers atop the wall. A few were so desperate to escape the beam of death they leaped from the wall hoping that they could survive the fall. They couldn't. The elegant white brick walls of Sylvannor still stood but now had a charred black line like a scar from where the dragon's breath landed. One of the great banners that depicted the Sylvan families symbol caught fire.

I got to my feet and surveyed the battlefield. A small portion of the surviving Blood Hawks were engaged in a melee battle with Dynam and the Storm Hunters while Terros aided them with his bow. The majority of the Blood Hawks, however, had turned their attention to the city walls. Cronus gave the signal and all four catapults launched their projectiles at the now weakened walls. The barrels of dragon dust all hit the wall and erupted into balls of fire. I could hear a loud crack as the integrity of the wall began to crumble. The Blood Hawks would breach the outer defenses in minutes if they weren't stopped.

I drew my ironwood blade and prepared to sneak up behind the Blood Hawks reloading the nearest catapult. I would die trying but perhaps I could manage to stop the assault on the walls. Suddenly I heard a blood-curdling scream to my left. I whirled around to see that six Blood Hawks had broken off from the main assault force and were now running toward the defenseless Storm

Hunters who were still slowly filling into the city.

Without a second thought, I tore off at a full sprint towards my people. I did not know if Rhea and Anthos were inside already or not but the fear that they might not be propelled me forward even faster. I gained ground quickly on the heavily armored Blood Hawks but they had a large lead. A few of the people in front took up knives and prepared to defend themselves but I knew they stood no chance.

I screamed at the top of my lungs to try and draw attention away from the innocent even going as far as too taunt the cowardly Blood Hawks. Two of them turned around to face me but I merely pushed them aside and continued forward. As the first Blood Hawk was about to bring his sword crashing down on an elderly man in front I dove forward and tackled him. I scrambled back to my feet and took a defensive stance in front of my people. The six Blood Hawks were no doubt caught off guard by the sudden appearance of a warrior. When they recovered, however, they did not hesitate to strike.

I deftly parried the first blow that came my way and kicked out at the Blood Hawk sending him sprawling backward. The next foe practically threw himself at me and I cleanly disarmed him and sent him back into the crowd of people behind me knowing they would overwhelm him.

Things carried on like this with my attackers

throwing strikes in my direction but none doing me any harm. When I felt confident enough, I leapt into the center of the remaining five and expertly slit two of their throats while parrying blows from the others. I continued to aggressively strike at my enemies cutting down another two leaving the final panicked Blood Hawk to desperately deflect my attacks. I pushed him back mercilessly until I plunged my blade straight into the armored chest of my foe.

I stood there surrounded by bodies and covered in the blood of my enemies. I was panting but I saw the shocked faces of my people and realized what I must look like. I scanned their faces and tried to control my breathing. Most were shocked or scared but a few gave slight nods of approval.

"Get inside," I said flatly. "Bar the gate."

They obeyed and I watched as they continued to file inside. One little boy even thanked me as he walked past. A smile escaped me and I couldn't help but feel extremely satisfied to have finally saved some lives.

I turned around to see that I was now quite a ways from the battlefield. Storm Hunters and Blood Hawks were locked in combat and their fight started to spill out of the forest and into the fields in front of the city. Small lines of fire from Vulcanor were beginning to trap a few unaware warriors who were too concentrated on their duels. I started to jog back just as Vulcanor came swooping in again delivering a killing blow to both Storm Hunters and Blood Hawks.

I saw Dynam and Terros engaged in a fight and decided to reinforce them. Dynam's chest and back were covered in small cuts and bruises. Terros appeared unscathed other than a limp. Blood stained the snow at their feet. They had each won their individual fights by the time I arrived and we stood back to back.

"We need to get inside the walls," Dynam said. "It's too dangerous out here with that dragon flying around."

I looked up at the creature who soared high in the sky. Vulcanor was the only one who had not sustained any damage, yet he undoubtedly had dealt the most death and destruction.

"That dragon has made this an even playing field," Terros said grimly. "We actually stand a chance against the Blood Hawks now."

I pursed my lips. Dynam and Terros both had good points. I tried to come up with some sort of plan that would give us even a chance of victory.

"Okay, we split up," I said. "Our people are too spread out right now and they're getting picked off. Try to rally as many as you can. We can push together to get inside the walls. And keep an eye on that dragon."

As I finished speaking, a Blood Hawk charged toward me. I defeated him with ease and when I turned around Dynam and Terros had already set out on their missions. I looked up again to see that Vulcanor was coming in fast and he seemed to have his target set on the weak point of the wall. I glanced at the wall and to my dismay, I saw Bevan standing there bravely commanding his men. The dragon inhaled and prepared to annihilate anyone who stood on that wall.

Get out of there! I wished I was close enough to warn him.

I gripped my sword until my knuckles turned white as I watched Bevan defiantly stare down the fearsome dragon barreling down at him. Just as the fiery breath left the dragon's crushing jaws an oversized crossbow bolt pierced its scales and landed deep in its shoulder. The dragon let out a terrible screech and lost control of where it was flying. The massive creature crashed into the wall beneath Bevan and the ground shook. A long crack traveled through the wall. A cloud of dust rose from where the beast lay and relief washed over me seeing the symbol of death lying there defeated. I looked to see that the bolt had come from one of the mounted crossbows. Bevan gave only a small nod of respect to the soldier who had saved his life.

I looked around me and noticed that Storm Hunters and Blood Hawks alike had temporarily halted the fighting to watch the spectacle. I made eye contact with a nearby enemy and he came at me wielding a spear. When I was finished with him I simply could not find any Storm Hunters to rally. I kept turning around and Blood Hawks continued to throw themselves at me. I fought them off but only barely. I was beginning to feel the extreme fatigue of extended battle. It became clear our plan was failing.

I caught a glimpse of Dynam in the distance and fought desperately to get to him but I was overwhelmed. I could not break through the waves of foes. I found myself side by side with two other hunters weary and wounded. The Blood Hawks had us completely surrounded and were closing in.

At that moment I heard a deafening roar that went on for what seemed like forever. The sheer volume caused me to drop to one knee. And sure enough, rising high into the sky, the bolt still protruding from his shoulder, was Vulcanor, the king of all dragons. The demon gained more height before circling around to rain fire on us again. I noticed that he was slower due to his wound, but no less deadly.

I used the distraction of the dragon to escape the closing circle of Blood Hawks. The hunters followed me but fell shortly after.

At this point, I was having a hard time finding any allies at all so I retreated to the forest. I saw on the right side of the battlefield, Dynam and Terros remained standing with a decent force of hunters behind them. They had succeeded in rallying our remaining men. As I scanned the field, another beam of fire came from the sky eviscerating a line of Blood Hawks. The gate to the city began to open and a small group of Sylvan warriors marched in perfect formation onto the battlefield. They formed a shield wall in front of them and began pushing the Blood Hawks back with their spears.

I stepped out of the forest and swiftly made my way towards Dynam hoping not to draw any attention until I got there. I watched as the Blood Hawks expertly divided their attention between the dragon, fighting my people, and the Sylvan reinforcements. I was nearing my allies when someone tackled me from the side. I swiftly rolled to my feet and held my sword at the ready. It took him longer to get up but when he did and I saw his face there was no mistaking his identity.

Cronus stood proudly in front of me. He gripped my father's blood-soaked blade tightly in his hand. Beads of sweat ran down his bald head and his breastplate was spotted with blood. His breathing was heavy and he looked at me with a ferocity that I'd never seen before.

Cronus came at me with powerful strikes that I had no hope of parrying. I dropped my bow to increase mobility and backpedaled clumsily trying to keep my distance. But Cronus did not let up. I threw my head back to avoid a decapitating blow and I could hear his blade cut through the air.

I backed into a Blood Hawk in my retreat. Cronus used the opportunity to punch me with the hilt of his sword. I fell to the ground. The taste of blood filled my mouth. Cronus continued to advance but I managed to swing my sword at his knee. I scrambled to my feet and his roar of pain told me all I needed to know.

I turned around having put a few feet between us and readied myself for his next attack. We danced around each other parrying and counter-attacking while the battle waged on all around us. No one dared to interrupt our duel. He swung at me and I deflected it. The shock from the forceful blow traveled up my sword and into my numb fingers. I slashed his hand with my next attack and he dropped his sword in pain.

Cronus drew a curved dagger and dove at me catching my wrist with the blade and causing me to lose my own weapon. We grappled in the dirt fighting over the dagger. Cronus was far stronger than me and it took only a moment for him to wrestle the blade away from me. I jerked my head to the side as he stabbed the cold dirt next to it.

He raised the dagger above his head and prepared to deal the killing blow. In a desperation move, I reached down and pressed my thumb hard into the wound I had given him on his knee earlier. He screamed in pain. I grabbed the dagger and jammed it deep into his stomach.

I shoved Cronus off of me and went quickly to retrieve my sword and my bow. I looked at my foe lying pitifully on the ground clutching the dagger that remained in his stomach. He pulled it out and blood flowed freely from the wound. I knew it would be fatal if not treated. Cronus got to his knees in front of me where he sat trying to muster words. We stared at each other for a long time almost in a separate world from the rest of the battle.

"Why, Cronus?" I asked. "Why did you kill my father?"

Cronus coughed up blood and spit it out before sneering.

"You are so selfish," he said. "You still think your father was some symbol of all things good."

"You aren't half the man he was," I replied. "My father would never do the things you've done."

"I protected my people!" Cronus retorted. "Something you've failed to do from the start."

I gritted my teeth. If he was trying to get under my skin, it was working. I nocked an arrow on my bow and drew the bowstring back aiming for him. It was time for me to end this.

Cronus chuckled.

"You talk all about your father's great sense of morality," Cronus said. "Yet here you stand ready to execute an unarmed man."

"I am not my father," I said my arms beginning to shake.

Cronus snorted. "No, your father was much easier to kill."

I glared at him down the shaft of the arrow that I could so easily end his life with. A bead of sweat rolled into my eye as I contemplated killing this man. All I had to do was let my fingers slip off the bowstring and it would put an end to all the war and suffering. And the man who was behind all the lies and murder would finally pay the price for his crimes. Cronus met my gaze. His eyes were angry but also tired. He seemed to goad me into doing it but I felt a strange pity for the man. I couldn't bring myself to kill him out of pure hatred.

A smile grew across Cronus face as I lowered my bow hesitantly.

"So you're not the same as he was after all," Cronus said quietly.

He seemed to have some strange sense of pride and accomplishment.

I tilted my head looking at my defeated enemy. I wondered if he would make some last attempt to wrestle my victory away from me. But no attack came and I began to question Cronus' motives. For the first time, his face did not hold malice. It was instead replaced with a sorrowful gaze. Perhaps he regretted some of the actions he had taken against my people.

"Chimera, look out!"

My eyes went to the walls of Sylvannor. I could see Bevan, a panicked look on his face. He was pointing toward the sky and when I followed his gesture I could see Vulcanor overhead swooping toward us. His jaws opened wide. Fire was building up in his throat. I'd immersed myself so completely in my battle with Cronus that I forgot about the greatest danger in this fight.

I found myself frozen in place as the flames barreled to the ground. My jaw dropped as the flames enveloped an unmoving Cronus in front of me, the same man that I had just decided to spare. He went smiling to his death and I felt a pang of grief but didn't know why. The beam of light continued toward me and I couldn't dodge it in time. Everything began to slow down and the memories of my family flashed before my eyes once again.

I knew I could not survive the heat blast but I had accomplished my mission. My people and most importantly my family were delivered safely to a place they could call home. Their only enemy I had just defeated. For the first time since my father died, I felt truly happy. I would die, but the Storm Hunters would live on within Sylvannor.

I looked to Bevan one last time and though I could see the sorrow in his eyes I knew we had won. I screamed out in pain as the flames engulfed my body. I could feel the excruciating pain of the flesh melting from my bones and I toppled over to the ground. I could faintly smell the sulfur before my senses dimmed and began to fade away. The pain went away, I closed my eyes, and after only a few moments, I drifted into the cold blackness of death.

10 - BROTHERS

I found myself standing in the Sylvan council chambers. Next to me were Dynam and Terros whose wounds were treated. Behind me sat my two siblings and a few other Storm Hunters. We were in the same booth that my father and I sat in not so long ago. I could not remember why my father was not with us. Syvos, Trofi, Caste, why were they not with us? There were twelve elevated chairs in front of us where the council members sat. There were, however, three empty chairs.

Bevan told me there was no time to fill me in on what was happening when I woke up. He mentioned that I may have lost my memory but I didn't care so much. I knew who my family and friends were so there wasn't much else that really mattered to me. The look on his face gave me chills.

To the right were the Blood Hawks, though there were far fewer than I thought there'd be. They were represented by a young boy who stood about half as tall as the rest of them. He wore the familiar armor of the Blood Hawks except with more decorative feathers signaling that he was their chieftain.

I was trying to recall recent events while Bevan addressed us. He caught my attention when he spoke my name.

"I have spoken to Chimera and Trostan," He gestured toward me and then the boy. "And they have both agreed to these terms."

I narrowed my eyes at Bevan, I did not remember coming to any sort of agreement.

"Due to the hideous crimes committed by Cronus Blood Hawk and his associates, and the ongoing rivalry between the Storm Hunters and the Blood Hawks…"

He paused to take a breath before continuing.

"The Sylvan families have ruled that it is only fair for the remaining Blood Hawks to vacate our lands within the next seven days."

I looked around at the smiling faces of my people. There was genuine joy and relief on their faces. On the other side of the room, the Blood Hawks didn't seem as upset as I would have thought. In fact, the boy, Trostan, nodded his head in agreement though he shot me a sidelong glance.

I could not recall why Cronus was no longer their chieftain. Perhaps he was preoccupied with other business. I would have to keep an eye out for him. I'd heard terrible stories about Cronus' brutality.

We began to shuffle out having been given the

council's decision. We made it into the hallway where Rhea and Anthos wanted to talk to me but I was uninterested in what they had to say. I needed to find Bevan so he could explain what was happening to me.

"You monster!"

I looked up to see Trostan running towards me, sword in hand. He was immediately grabbed and held back by the guards. I looked at him with a blank stare. Why did he have such animosity towards me?

"You killed my father!" He screamed as they dragged him away. "You murdered him!"

And then it all came rushing back to me. I remembered Cronus' ambushing and killing my father. I remembered our attack on the Blood Hawks camp and the permanent scars dealt to Apistos. And I pictured in vivid detail, my duel with Cronus, Vulcanor's rampage, and my own death at the hands of the dragon. This reality I was in now suddenly seemed so real. It wasn't a dream yet I also knew I couldn't have possibly survived.

I winced as I felt a sharp pain centered around the scar on my left arm. I was beginning to feel lightheaded and the pain in my arm only intensified. I spun around wildly and noticed the worried and confused looks on my sibling's faces. I fell to my knees in the middle of the crowd and cried out for help as my arm began to feel as though it were falling off. The pain was so severe and I could actually feel the heat emanating from the scar on my face. And then the pain suddenly stopped and I felt a cold chill travel down my spine before I passed out.

* * *

When I awoke, I was lying on a cot in a small living area. I sat up slowly and took in my surroundings. Across the room was a small desk and behind me was a small staircase that led to an upper level. I heard footsteps above but did not know who they belonged to. To my right, I could see a small balcony and on it was Bevan. I must've been in his home.

I got to my feet and made my way to him. The small home sat on top of a tower along the right outer wall of the city so the balcony gave us a view of everything. We looked over the city in silence together for a few moments. I could see that in the fields in front of the city many people still worked to remove the dead. In the center of it all was the carcass of Vulcanor. I could see at least four large bolts protruding from his corpse but it could've taken more to fell the king of dragons.

"I remember everything, now," I said. "After Trostan said I murdered his father, it all came back to me. He'll never know that I chose to spare Cronus."

A single tear escaped me and I turned my head to wipe it away.

"Is this real?" I asked. "Am I really still alive?"

Bevan hesitated. "Yes, this is real, and logically that would mean you are alive, though even I don't know how that's possible. I watched with my own eyes as the dragon's breath burned you alive and now here you stand without even a burn mark to show for it."

"I don't remember anything after, well, after my death."

"Once the battle had ended and we began cleaning up the bodies, I saw you. You were on the ground, wounded, but not dead. I brought you in and cleaned you up and your injuries healed with miraculous speed. The whole time you were mumbling and asking the same questions over and over. I was worried your memory was truly damaged."

I rolled up my sleeve to reveal the phoenix scar once again.

"We never knew what power this scar held, but now I think we do."

Bevan raised his eyebrows.

"You think the scar brings the gift of immortality?"

"Perhaps, or at least the power to stave off death once. There's no other explanation for why I remember dying. And when my memories came back I experienced the pain of my death a second time. All the pain emanates directly from this scar."

Bevan took a deep breath and contemplated

what I just said.

"Then our only remaining question is why."

"Why what?"

"Why were you and I chosen to carry the gift that is these scars and the immortality that follows?"

I shook my head. "Were we given this as a gift? Or are we cursed to outlive all our loved ones."

"I don't believe that," Bevan said kindly.

We stood there in silence. A cool breeze blew against my face as I closed my eyes and took a deep breath.

"Cronus said I wasn't like my father when I decided to spare him. What did he mean by that?" I asked.

Bevan sighed and looked away. I frowned and tilted my head.

"I swore to Andras I would never tell anyone."

"Please, Bevan, my father and Cronus are both dead. If you know something I don't, I beg you to tell me."

Bevan leaned on the railing and looked over the edge. He weighed his choices, either keep his promise to his dead friend or tell the truth.

"Your father only ever wanted to protect you."

I waited patiently for Bevan to muster the courage to say it. Finally, he stood straight again and spoke.

"Cronus was your uncle, Chimera. He was your father's younger brother."

I stared straight ahead not knowing what to say. My heart was pounding in my chest and I felt my face turn red. The man who caused me so much grief was my uncle? I looked for a way to disprove it.

"Then why would he murder my father?"

"The story you've been told is that one day Cronus went crazy and killed your grandparents so he could take over your grandfather's position as chieftain. When he failed to kill Andras, he was forced to run and that's when he created the Blood Hawks."

I nodded understanding so far.

"But that story is entirely a fiction. Growing up together, Andras and Cronus were not close. This was due in part to their abusive parents. Andras began to hate Cronus because he wasn't treated as harshly as he was. One day, after one too many beatings, Andras lashed out and killed both of their parents. That was when Cronus decided to form his own tribe because he couldn't stand to even look at his brother. Andras framed Cronus for their parent's murder and so the lines were drawn. The Storm Hunters who believed Andras. And the Blood Hawks who believed Cronus."

I held my head in my hands. I was at a complete loss for words. With my eyes closed, I could imagine the scene playing out and I hated every second of it. I didn't want to believe it but Bevan had no reason to lie.

"I believe Cronus originally intended to wipe you all out. But through some twisted line of thinking, he thought he could save you."

"How could my father do something so evil?" I asked.

"What Andras did is inexcusable, though I don't know if it could be called evil," Bevan said. "The details of the past neither of us will ever truly know. All we can do is move forward."

"How does one move on from this?" I asked.

"We just do, Chimera. We still have responsibilities to our people. That is the nature of leadership. We put on a face of bravery to help others get through what we cannot."

Bevan's words encouraged me though I still had doubts. We stood there together, two leaders overlooking our city.

"Will you be moving your people to your new plot of land?"

I stood looking over the beautiful city thinking about his question.

"No," I said. "That land represents the war and everything I hate about it."

Bevan nodded. "I thought you might say that. There's a castle called Parath on the Silver Sea not terribly far from here. It was abandoned by the Sylvan Families long ago and has fallen into disrepair. With some care, it could be returned to its former glory and become the new home of the Storm Hunters."

I nodded. "I'd like that."

"Then we should get to work. Rebuilding is the hard part."

I nodded. "Thank you, Bevan, for everything."

* * *

I entered the small home that I would be staying in for the next few weeks until Bevan told us our new castle was ready. It was bigger than I expected it to be two or three times as big as Bevan's home. Anthos, Rhea, and Dynam followed me into the building. Anthos immediately ran to find his new room.

"Bevan said he would set us up in one of the coastal forts they abandoned when the Blood Hawks formed," I said. "We would need to do some maintenance but it has walls."

"That's better than anything we've had before," Rhea said.

Dynam nodded. "A fresh start."

Rhea and Dynam, despite their hopeful words, seemed restless.

"I know it's going to be hard to get on with our normal lives, but we have to try," I said putting on the brave face Bevan had told me about.

"It's not the first time I've had to rebuild my life," Dynam said. "If you need any pointers…"

He gestured to himself and I chuckled.

"I know I failed you both at different points through this war, but if you accept it, I'd love the opportunity to try to be your chieftain again."

"I would like nothing more," Dynam said.

"You're the only one who can be," Rhea said. "At least, the only one who father would want to be."

I nodded and took a deep breath. I'd made mistakes, I knew that. But I couldn't be surrounded by a more forgiving group of people.

"What happened outside the council chambers?" Dynam asked. "Was that related to the battle?"

I weighed in my mind how much I wanted to tell them. Surely it would be shocking news. I shook my head. They deserved to know the truth just like I did.

"Yes, Bevan and I were talking. There are a few things I need to tell you two about the phoenix scar."

ABOUT THE AUTHOR

Ben Caskey has always been interested in a good story. Growing up on books and movies in the fantasy sci-fi genre, he wanted to take on the challenge of telling a story set in these fantastical worlds. Chimera is his first attempt to do just that. To learn more about Ben or how to purchase his books visit BenCaskey.com

47463534R00111

Made in the USA
Middletown, DE
07 June 2019